FOLLOW
YOUR
DREAM

FOLLOW YOUR DREAM

BY

Marjorie Holmes

The Westminster Press

PHILADELPHIA

For Bobbie Olsen

whose gay and patient help
enabled me to write this book

Chapter 1

THE GIRL in the back row gnawed her nails. The girl in the back row sputtered, beat her fists against her knees, and threshed futilely about.

"Hey, lookit Tracey!" one of the senior boys whispered to the pretty thing sitting beside him, and she giggled and poked a friend. Word rippled up and down the aisles: "Watch Tracey Temple — she's about to explode!"

It was a pleasant diversion from the speaker. Career Day speakers could be pretty dismal. Actually, this guy, a vet, lounging on the podium with his hands in his pockets, cracking jokes, wasn't as abysmal as some. A little too buddy-buddy maybe, and when he got serious, naturally all he could interest were a few of the brighter boys.

The only girl who was paying any attention to him, now that he was describing the unutterable joys of attending an expectant cow or setting a dog's tail, was Tracey. And her reactions were so gloriously, threateningly in character that they furnished delicious relief.

"But I say again and I can't say it too often — veterinary medicine is no place for a girl!"

He had said it once too often. To the vast joy of the

whole assembly, it happened as hoped — Tracey Temple
was on her feet. And her shirttail was out, as usual, and
her dusty blond hair, which spurted all over her head like
feathers — when it got in her way she just grabbed a
pair of scissors and whacked it off, the kids claimed —
seemed almost to bristle, and her rich voice rang out like
the alarm for a fire drill. " Why not? " she demanded. The
voice was shaking a little, but that only enlisted their
sympathies. " Please tell us why, Dr. McDowell. Surely a
profession so — so *maternal* as you make it sound ought to
be a natural for a woman! "

There was a roar of laughter as the speaker flung up a
hand to ward off this blow. Obviously maternal was the
last word he cared to have associated with this lusty
calling.

The hearty young man with the black-rimmed glasses
rallied. " Because," he said with a mixture of firmness,
good humor, and condescension, " it's too tough, too
strenuous. It's a man's job for a real he-man who's willing
to work," he flagrantly courted the boys. " Women just
don't have the qualifications."

Tracey was clutching the seat ahead of her, but she
held her ground. " How about some of the women who've
proved otherwise? " she persisted. " How about the
president of the District of Columbia Academy of Veterinary Medicine, Dr. Jane Baldwin? "

The speaker made a small hopeless gesture as if to say,
" What do you do about such a dame? " and the kids
laughed again, halfway on his side now.

" I'd rather not go into personalities," he said. " In fact,
I'd hoped we'd wait till the question-and-answer period
to go into this sort of thing."

Mr. Scoggins, the principal, had sprung up too. " Yes,
indeed. May I apologize for this unfortunate interrup-

10

tion?" He glared at Tracey, who stood quaking but grim. "There will be no more questions until our guest has finished. Dr. McDowell, will you proceed?"

Tracey gave a little gulp. Angrily she went crawling over knees and stumbling over feet to reach the aisle. "Atta girl, Tracey," some of the fellows cheered. And, "You tell 'em, kid."

But safe in the girls' rest room she gave way to tears. "Talk about democracy! Talk about freedom of speech!" she appealed furiously to the first girl who hastened to her side at the shrilling of the dismissal bell.

"I know, Trace, I know," soothed her oldest and dearest friend, Liz Cadell. "But we were proud of you."

"That's right, Trace." The other girls trooped in, lending their support as they began freshening lipstick, combing hair. She was an oddball, sure. A girl who preferred the company of animals to human beings, imagine! And who wrote papers like, "Brucellosis, a Disease that Costs the American Farmer a Hundred Million Dollars a Year," and walked off with top honors at the Science Fair. How could you really talk to a girl like that? What could you share?

Yet they adored her. She was cute, with her gamin face, which was always deeply sun-tanned and looked striking with her near-white, crazy hair. She was so odd they felt protective toward her. And she was funny. There was something comical about her very intensity, and something exhilarating. When she stalked out of class or sprang up to challenge a speaker, their own submerged rebellions responded. The nerve of her!

Still, brushing off their half-amused, half-commiserating plaudits, Tracey trudged miserably home. She'd looked forward to meeting the speaker, had actually had notions of broaching the subject of a job this summer. But no, she'd had to open her big mouth. Not that it would've done

11

any good to ask him, a guy as prejudiced as that.

She hoped to heaven the principal didn't call her mother. Mom was worried enough about her already. Poor Mother! The ghost of an ache haunted Tracey's heart. However Mom tried to hide it, she must be disappointed. A woman as pretty as Mother ought to have a frilly daughter, a girl who was at least as interested in dates as dogs. Her mother had been a wonderful sport, considering — going far above and beyond the call of duty, to make up, Tracey supposed, for Tracey's not having a father.

Everything Mother had ever done, actually, had been for her. Taking that job on the Carter ranch in Wyoming to cook and clean for all those boys after Tracey's father had been killed when she was two. Nostalgia gripped her as she remembered — the mountains, the waterfall, and the ponies. She'd had her own pinto to ride before she was five. And she remembered the boys who she'd thought for a long time were her brothers — Clem and Rick and Bill and Jeff. Jeff had been her favorite, and had taught her to ride.

She'd cried, she remembered, when she found out they weren't even related. "Not even Jeff?" she had pleaded. And Mother had sat on her bunk, trying to explain.

"But they're almost like brothers, darling — like having your own family. That's why we came out here."

Even moving to Washington ten years ago had been, Tracey realized, for her sake. Mom had finally decided it wasn't so good, after all, raising one girl among all those boys. She'd studied nights and practiced up on her short-hand and taken a Civil Service exam, which brought her back to Washington, where Grandma Temple lived, and a job with the FBI.

Tracey had been literally ill with loneliness for the ranch and the boys and her dog and cat and all the horses. Of

12

all her pets, the only one she could bring along was a horned toad, Hoppy, and he had died. It was in sheer desperation, she supposed, that Mother had begun letting her keep other things, until the menagerie had grown to its present size.

When they'd signed the lease to the apartment they shared with Grandma there hadn't been any clause about pets. But new management had taken over during the last year, and the rule that no animals would be tolerated was generally understood.

Keeping things under control had become a strain. The three women lived in a constant state of suspense. And today, when Tracy came storming in, the blow fell.

"Tracey," her grandmother announced in tones both excited and dramatic, "the jig is up. They've found out! The manager will be up in a few minutes to investigate." She was an immense, regal woman, with a pompadour of glistening white hair, real pearls, which she wore day and night, a flowered smock, and a cane.

"Oh, brother! That's all I need. Well, let's go!"

Flinging down her books, Tracey began grabbing cages, at the same time giving the quick series of kicks on the wall that signaled Dudley Wallace. She and Dudley had learned Morse code together when they were just little kids, and for years they'd communicated. But they'd agreed that in times of real emergency a few swift kicks were quicker and just as effective.

She only hoped Dudley wasn't lingering downstairs discussing the chemotherapy of leukemia or something lively like that with old Mrs. Busby, who had a Ph.D. and liked to be called "doctor" and discuss erudite-sounding things.

With a cage of white mice in one hand, Tracey threw up the kitchen window. Good! The pulley platform was already in place, as planned. Loading it with the mice; Ike, the alligator; five noisily chattering parakeets; and Cricket, the Boston terrier, who wasn't a bit afraid and seemed to enjoy the ride, Tracey was infinitely glad they'd practiced. She and Dudley had shipped all the members of her menagerie back and forth often enough to get them used to it. Thank goodness none of them got airsick, except Ornrietta, the cat, and they had lived so long in danger of discovery that they knew better than to set up a fuss.

Now if Dudley were only there! " Hey, Dudley! " Tracey kicked the wall again and hollered.

To her immense relief, his blond crew cut and glasses poked promptly out. Dudley was really nothing to look at — his neck was too long and his cheek bones were rugged — but at the moment Dudley looked beautiful indeed.

" This is it! " Tracey told him grimly. " Grab 'em fast and haul 'em in while I gather up some more."

" O. K." Dudley swallowed a last bite of cake, dusted his hands of crumbs, and began to pull. " Where're the hamsters? "

" Hibernating. In the refrigerator. I don't really think he'll look in there. Do you, Gammy? " she consulted the huge figure, who was lumbering about frantically spraying the air with Arpege perfume. " But we'd better get the guinea pigs out of the kitchen cupboards — they might get to scratching."

" Yes, by all means. Yes," averred the grandmother firmly, squirting more perfume furiously in her direction. " Guinea pigs are so dumb. You just can't train them. I've always thought how nice it is that guinea pigs can't bark."

" That reminds me! Where's Littlebit? " Tracey plumped a load of squirming guinea pigs into a box, hoisted it onto the sill, and began looking under things. " Here, Littlebit! Here, Littlebit! "

14

"Poor little thing. She's frightened — she senses danger," The grandmother cuddled the miniature poodle which had leaped quivering into her arms. "Wait, I'll get my pocketbook. She's used to that and she won't make a sound, will you, sweetheart? She'll just think we're taking her to the park for an airing."

Grabbing a huge beaded bag from a drawer, she stuffed the small dog into it and snapped the catch. "Thank goodness you got rid of that Saint Bernard!" she chuckled.

"Hey, hurry up over there!" they could hear Dudley warning. "And where're Eloise and Ambrose? They find those snakes you'll be out on the street for sure."

"That's right!" Tracey dashed back to her bedroom, only to find the cages empty. "Where are they? Quick, Gammy! I hear somebody coming. Did you let Eloise and Ambrose out this afternoon?"

"Oh, my goodness!" The old woman's hand went to her open mouth. "They're in the bathroom — I think. I remember putting them in the tub to clean out their cages, and then the telephone rang — " she made quickly for the bathroom door.

Tracey got there first, and her heart sank. The white porcelain tub was empty. And a quick survey revealed no sleek black bodies anywhere. The two women faced each other, and then turned with one accord to survey the tub once more. The plug was definitely not in the hole.

"Oh, Grandma!" Tracey wailed, torn between exasperation and anguish. "Two beautiful snakes that I've raised from babies down the drain!"

"I know, dear, I know, and I can't tell you how sorry I am. But at least it solves one problem for the moment," she reasoned. "And," she added timidly, "they may turn up."

"Yes, in somebody else's bathtub!" The ghastly possi-

15

bility presented itself. The apartment house was filled mostly with little old ladies, or maiden ones. And people, especially ladies, had this silly prejudice against snakes. They screamed at the sight of little green grass snakes, let alone long, lovely black ones like Ambrose and Eloise. Why, even Mother, who was really amazingly tolerant, had been quite provoked that time she was having bridge club and Ambrose insisted on getting on the bed and nosing around the women's hats. Thank goodness none of the guests had spotted him! As Mom pointed out, one of them might have had a heart attack.

No, plainly this was serious. Still, their disappearance had its fortuitous side right now. And feeling like a traitorous mother locking her children out, Tracey jammed the plug back in, so they couldn't come back till the danger was past.

" I'll send over the empty cages," she informed Dudley, " And Littlebit's in Gammy's bag. If she starts to yip, give her a bottle."

" Honestly! A dog six months old and not weaned yet! " scolded Dudley good-humoredly.

Tracey felt a pang of maternal embarrassment. Littlebit was spoiled, no doubt of that. But, after all, what could you do when a puppy started to whimper every time the janitor came snooping around? And poodles were smart. Littlebit had taken shameless advantage of the precarious situation.

Tracey slammed down the window as footsteps rapped down the hall. Together with her grandmother she took final frantic inventory. Too late to do anything about, she saw the bird droppings that trailed down the spectacles of Grandpa Temple's portrait over the mantle, and a stain on the carpet where Littlebit hadn't gotten to the paper in time. But the air reeked of Arpege perfume instead of live-

16

stock, and except for two tanks of leisurely swimming tropical fish, the premises were petless. All you could do now was hope.

The footsteps halted. A key turned in the lock. " Mom! " Tracey shouted in her relief. Then she noticed her mother's tight lips as she jerked off her gloves and threw down her pert small hat.

"They called me at work," Ellen Temple announced. " They said, ' We understand you're raising chinchillas.' "

" Chinchillas? " Grandmother Temple looked at Tracey in innocent mystification. Nothing had ever surprised her, and nothing ever would.

" Chinchillas! " whooped Tracey. " Not really? "

" Well, they wouldn't be any worse than what we have." Mrs. Temple whipped off her suit coat now — a smart little blue jacket with a lining that matched her blouse. She always stripped down for action when she was upset, and it was kind of awe-inspiring to see a woman so little and so pretty so aroused. Her hair, the exact white-gold color of Tracey's, was swept smartly back into a French twist. Her eyes, a lively, burning brown, were like Tracey's too, but there the resemblence ended. Where Mrs. Temple was petite and poised and exquisitely feminine, Tracey was a hoyden, brash, tactless, and so utterly absorbed in her private passions that when it came to clothes she couldn't care less.

" Tracey, I simply cannot stand it any longer! All this secrecy, this skulking about and hiding. It's — deceitful, a — a disgrace. I know, I know, it's my fault," she forestalled Tracey's defense. " I've been too lenient — I didn't want you to be lonely. Well, I see I've been wrong. There are rules against animals in apartment houses, and we've got to abide by them the same as everyone else."

" There weren't any rules when we moved in."

17

"Well, there are now. This new management —" Her mother glanced around, frowning. "By the way, where are the beasts?"

"Dudley's," said Tracey meekly, heart hammering at the determination in her mother's manner. You could push her only so far.

"Well, we are simply going to admit the truth to the manager when he comes up, and then get rid of them."

"Not Littlebit!" cried Tracey. "Not Cricket and Ornrietta!"

Her mother flinched slightly, but she said: "Yes, every blessed one if he insists. You know how hard apartments are to find, especially anything we can afford. And nobody else would take us with this — this zoo!"

The knocker rapped smartly. The three women exchanged anxious glances. Then Mrs. Temple marched to the door with shoulders back.

Chapter 2

MR. ABBOTT, the new manager, was a large, florid, genial man, full of gallant apologies. "I'm sorry, but we've had some complaints. I've come to investigate this report about your daughter's raising chinchillas, Mrs. Temple."

"Chinchillas?" To Tracey's immense joy and pride, her mother was the picture of composure. "Why, that's ridiculous!"

"Yes, it does seem slightly — preposterous." He laughed, as nervous as the little group itself. "I'm sure you won't mind if I just have a look around?"

"Oh, my no!" said Mrs. Temple. "Go right ahead."

Tracey could have hugged her mother. For the moment,

18

at least, she was not to be betrayed. But her knees were sick with apprehension. She thought of the water pans under the sink, the leashes behind the door, the puppy biscuits, and for that matter evidence of guinea pigs in the cupboards. And perish forbid that Mr. Abbott be inspired to open the refrigerator! If a mere mother couldn't get over being startled to find hamsters hobnobbing with her milk and eggs, you could hardly expect a total stranger not to go into mild shock.

As for Ambrose and Eloise — Grandma was often absent-minded. What if, instead of the bathtub, she'd put those snakes on the buffet or maybe a dressing table?

"Well, well — " Mr. Abbott had paused in Tracey's bedroom, and her heart was in her mouth. "The young lady does have a definite interest in animals, doesn't she? I can tell that by her books."

"Oh, yes, indeed!" Ellen Temple's voice was light; she cast a fond if despairing glance at Tracey. "From the time she was small. It's sort of — frustrating. Whenever I ask her what she wants for her birthday or graduation, instead of jewelry or something nice to wear, I get a request for a book on sheep husbandry or — anthrax! She thinks she wants to be a vet."

Tracey's chin jutted. "I'm going to be a vet."

"Why?" Mr. Abbott seemed amused.

"Because I love animals," Tracey blurted. "And talk about frustrating. It's frustrating to me not to have a place where I can keep all I want. Not just a little apartment where I can't manage anything but dogs and cats and hamsters and snakes and things like that, but — " She caught herself, aghast.

There was a moment of frozen silence. Then Mr. Abbott grinned weakly. "What — no chinchillas?"

"No." Tracey laughed too, albeit desperately. "No

19

chinchillas — I swear it. But, please, Mr. Abbott, if I can just keep Cricket and Littlebit — the poodle and the terrier. They're small dogs, beautifully trained. They never bark — you'd never know they were here. They never bother anybody — "

At that instant there was a muted but definite howl from next door, a howl that mounted in pitch as the silence thickened. Then tramp, tramp, tramp, and a hammering at the door.

"Is it safe?" Dudley's blond crop poked in. "Is the old buzzard gone? We're outta milk, and this spoiled brat bit me when I tried to make her suck my fingers." He blanched, then flamed scarlet. "Oh — you, Mr. Abbott!"

The inventory took quite a while. Mr. Abbott could scarcely believe it himself. He kept saying: "Well, of course I'm new to this job — I've only been here six months. But — six months! And you say you've been smuggling these dogs to the park for how many months?"

"Well, not these dogs exactly." Grandmother Temple stopped to calculate. "There was the time she had the Saint Bernard. It was a stray that she took in and mothered, but we did become so attached to it, even if it did knock over lamps and chew up the rugs. I do believe that was the most difficult time."

"No, Mother, wouldn't you say the most difficult time was when she had the goat?" Ellen Temple asked, straight-faced. She had a wicked sense of humor sometimes, and she could resort to it to bolster Tracey's sagging spirits. "It was a very *small* goat," she informed Mr. Abbott. "And all it ate was the towels. Of course this was long before you came," she hastily assured him. "Before we — well — knew about any rules."

20

The manager laughed doubtfully, mopped his brow, and went on writing. "You understand I don't make these regulations," he pointed out. "It's just my job to enforce them." He turned to Tracey, who slumped fiercely on the couch, legs outstretched, arms grimly folded. "I'm honestly sorry, Miss Tracey."

But Tracey was not to be appeased. "Men!" she raged when he had gone and she and Dudley were racing back and forth transferring the livestock. "They're all alike. Pigheaded and stupid, scared of any girl who threatens their precious authority or gives them any competition. Like that blind, stupid veterinarian — only I hate to give him the dignity of the name — who spoke at school today."

"Hey, watch it!" Dudley protested, grinning. "You're talking about the sex to which I belong."

"That's right, Tracey," her mother warned. "You sound pretty blind and stupid yourself when you talk like that."

"All I can say is it's a shame boys have to grow up to become them!" Tracey slammed down the last caged parakeet. "He wouldn't even discuss Dr. Baldwin," she informed her mother indignantly, catching up Littlebit and taking some comfort in the eager nuzzling of her cold nose, the caress of the rough little red tongue. "Here right down in Georgetown we've got one of the best women vets in the world, and he's got the nerve to stand there and say women don't belong!"

"Yes, dear, we're well aware of your great admiration for Dr. Baldwin." Her mother was hopelessly surveying the agglomeration of cages, boxes, and baskets of scrambling, chortling animals. "But we've got an immediate problem to solve. You'd better call the pet store right now and see how much they'll buy. Heaven knows we

21

can use the money for college."

"Not Littlebit, not Cricket!" Tracey passionately protested.

"Maybe you could turn them over to Liz. After all, they've a big yard and live close. You could go over to feed and care for them every day — it'd be almost the same thing."

"If you'll help me build the shelves, I'll take the hamsters and some of the mice," volunteered Dud. "We'll put 'em over in that garage I rented for my leukemia experiments. All but the alligator," he added. "I hate to say this, but I don't really think Ike is a very congenial guy."

"Speaking of alligators reminds me —" Grandma Temple began to root around the papers on the telephone stand. "Tracey, Great-aunt Azalea called."

"Mother, really!" Ellen remonstrated, with a little laugh.

"No offense. It's just that she has such hideous taste — those incredible hats and that alligator bag. Yes, it's the bag — every time I see that alligator on her bag I wish I weren't so fat. I declare it looks as if it's positively licking its chops. Oh, yes, here's the number. She says she can be reached here till six. After that she'll be home. Azalea!" she exclaimed with sudden inspiration. "Why not let her take Ornrietta? You know how she is about cats."

Hearing her name, Ornrietta began to wind in and out between Tracey's legs, then sprang to her shoulder. Tracey nuzzled the black rumbling bundle as she dialed. She'd found Ornrietta mewing plaintively around the trash barrels one night, a lost and half-starved kitten. Surely, oh, surely they wouldn't be so cruel as to deprive her of Ornrietta.

"Dr. Baldwin's office."

Tracey was so startled she nearly dropped the phone. Though she shouldn't have been, if she'd considered. Dr. Baldwin had always looked after Aunt Azalea's cats. It was from Great-aunt Azalea, in fact, that she'd first heard of the distinguished woman vet and become her idolizing fan. Once, quaking, she'd personally transported Golden Boy, Aunt Azalea's prize Persian, to Dr. Baldwin's for boarding. But the great woman had been upstairs operating, and Tracey had had to come away without even getting a glimpse, let alone her autograph.

"I — oh! I was told I might reach Miss Azalea Courtney at this number."

"I'm sorry, Miss Courtney has left," the receptionist said. "But I wonder — is this her niece? If so, Dr. Baldwin would like to speak with you."

Dr. Baldwin speak with *her?* Tracey gripped the table's edge. Her heart began to beat so hard she could scarcely answer when another voice, low and rich, rather clipped and firm but friendly too, asked: "Is this Tracey Temple? Your aunt was telling me you're interested in working this summer, and it happens I'm short of help. I wonder if you'd like to come in for an interview."

"Would I?" Tracey shrieked. Then, recovering her aplomb: "Oh, my goodness, yes! Yes, indeed, Dr. Baldwin, any time you say."

"All right, let's make it Monday then, around three."

"O.K., fine! Wonderful! I'll be there!" Tracey assured her, recklessly dismissing the fact that she didn't even get out of her last class till five of. "And — and thank you, thank you so much!"

Dazedly she hung up. Still trying to take in this amazing windfall, she stood regarding the frankly curious faces in the room. Then, with a bloodcurdling war whoop,

23

Tracey began to hug everyone in sight: mother, grandmother, animals — even Dudley.

"Tracey, where are you going?"

Tracey was brought up short as she hastened down the hall. It was Mr. Scoggins, the principal, and even when she showed him her special permission slip to leave school early, he insisted on marching her into his office for a talk. By the time he got through telling her how brilliant she was (three minutes), but how disrupting an influence (three more), and that you can't go through life making your own rules (five), it was eighteen minutes till three o'clock.

"Yes, sir," and, "No, sir," she kept meekly replying, if only to shut him off. But Mr. Scoggins was a man who became more deeply enamored of his message the longer he talked. He was giving her the good-example routine now, and having been through this several times, Tracey knew it would continue for several minutes more.

"Please!" she broke in desperately. "I'm sorry, but this is vital. I'm having an interview that may mean a job — with Dr. Baldwin!"

"Who's Dr. Baldwin?"

Tracey was aghast. This was tantamount to admitting he'd never heard of people like Louis Pasteur or Madame Curie or Dr. Jonas Salk. Plainly it would be futile to try to set him straight. Besides, there wasn't time.

"Mr. Scoggins, please, I'm already late. I'll miss my bus!"

Knowing it was now or never, she made a dash for it, colliding with one teacher and barely missing another as she burst through the swinging doors. Well, the worst they could do to her was give her some more detention slips, she reasoned, racing down the steps. Certainly

24

nothing could be as bad as being late and maybe losing out on this wonderful opportunity.

Compensation, maybe that's what it was! Maybe, as Emerson said, for every awful thing that happens to you, there's something good to make up for it. All weekend it had seemed that nothing could compensate for the empty cages, for having to leave Littlebit crying like a baby for her, despite all the bottles Liz, bless her heart, could warm. For going to bed without Ornrietta rumbling like a warm little steamboat in her arms. For the heavy, sickening silence in the apartment where before there had been scratching and chirping and the patter of little paws.

But she had been bolstered by this strong, shining rod of hope. To get a job with a vet — just any old vet — would have been perfect, but actually to see and know and work with the famous Dr. Jane Baldwin! Well, it was almost too much to dare to think about.

The bus was just lumbering around the corner as Tracey raced down the hill. "Wait, wait!" she screamed futilely, knowing that since nobody was standing at the bus stop it would sail right on. To her anguish, that's what happened: she had to stand with sinking heart, watching its taunting little blue tail of fumes disappear. It would be at least fifteen minutes before another came along, and a taxi was out of the question. Maybe if she climbed the hill to the drugstore and phoned and said she'd be a little late — But she shrank from such an admission right off. No, the best thing would be to walk a few blocks over and catch a bus there; they ran more often.

She had worn heels, albeit small ones, hoping to look a little more sophisticated and older, but they made walking hard. After the first block, Tracey took them off and streaked toward her destination in stocking feet. A bus was coming. Still carrying the shoes, Tracey clambered on.

25

It wasn't until she'd deposited her books on the seat and was getting back into her shoes that she noticed people looking at her, and heard a woman remark: "These teen-agers! Honestly! They seem to get wilder all the time."

Tracey flushed, not knowing whether to be mad or amused. About the wildest thing she'd ever done was stay up all night with Dud once catching frogs. Still, she didn't want Dr. Baldwin getting the wrong impression. Anxiously she began poking locks of her mop of white-blond hair behind her ears and putting on the gloves her mother had laid out that morning. When they got nearer she might even wear the tiny pearl earrings in her purse.

The bus made agonizingly slow progress. People got on at every stop, and then to make everything just peachy, they were delayed by an accident on the corner ahead. She'd be late, and there was no help for it — it was already after three. And now she began to worry about where she was supposed to transfer. Gammy had taken down the directions from Aunt Azalea, arguing about them at the time, Tracey remembered. And since it was a draw as to which of them could be the more rattled or absent-minded, they could both be wrong.

Tracey decided to ask the driver, but he'd gotten off to see how long they'd be held up. She couldn't get his attention. She decided to walk on to K Street and get a Georgetown bus there. The instructions on the paper said you could.

Hopefully, Tracey got on. But they kept turning corners and going past Government buildings, and nothing looked like Georgetown as she remembered it at all. And when she saw the Capitol looming before her in all its majesty, the hideous truth dawned. She'd been riding all this time in the wrong direction! And it was now nearly four o'clock.

In sheer desperation she'd have taken a taxi now, except

for the fact that she had barely bus fare home. Again she considered calling Dr. Baldwin to explain the minute she got off. But there weren't any drugstores handy up here around the Capitol grounds.

Distraught, Tracey sought directions from a policeman, who patiently steered her across the street to the proper island. And again the slow journey and the complicated business of transferring began.

She simply didn't seem to be able to get there, that was all. This was a kind of fiendish punishment for her many sins: being rude to Mr. Scoggins, and saying men were awful, and snapping at Dudley lots of times, and getting out of the dishes, and being such a disappointment to Mother, and maybe even for the long deception of keeping pets in the apartment. No, no, this was but her slow eternal doom — to go riding forever around Washington in search of a wildly longed for goal that must be forever and eternally just beyond her reach.

"Twenty-ninth Street," the driver barked, jerking his head to catch her eye in the mirror. "Didn't you say this is where you wanted to get off?"

"Oh, yes, yes, thank you." She stumbled down the steps. The doors sucked shut behind her, and there it was. On the corner. A white-brick, vine-covered building. A door painted midnight blue. And over it a sign saying: DR. JANE BALDWIN. ANIMAL HOSPITAL.

Disheveled, perspiring, breathless, ashamed, Tracey dragged timidly in. On blue-leather chairs in the pine-paneled waiting room people sat restraining a variety of dogs, while two women held cats and a caged parrot that kept waddling back and forth croaking: "Hey, you, gimme a kiss! Hey, you!"

At the desk a plump, sweet-faced woman with a friz of gray bang and glasses was trying to answer the telephone

27

and also speak into the intercommunication system. Beside her, holding a monkey, stood the tallest, handsomest, and quite the most terrifying man Tracey had ever seen.

"Yes?" he snapped at her, since the receptionist was so obviously occupied. "What do you want?"

"I — I'm Tracey Temple." Her tongue was dry — it would hardly work. "Dr. Baldwin asked me to — to —" The rest of it stuck sickeningly in her throat.

"My dear child —" The receptionist flashed a puzzled glance her way. "It's nearly five o'clock. You were expected at three!"

"I got held up at school. Then I — got lost." It was a dumb and appalling thing to have to admit. Especially with that revoltingly handsome male staring contemptuously at you.

"Well, Doctor's having office hours right now. I don't know — I'll see." The receptionist pressed a buzzer, announced for all to hear, "That girl finally showed up, Doctor." In a second she inclined her head. "She says for you to take her back, Whit, and have her wait."

A cocker on its owner's lap began to tug frantically at its leash and yap at her as she passed. The parrot, swinging upside down on its perch, yelled caustically: "Hey, good-lookin', gimme a kiss! Hey, you!" And to add insult to injury, the monkey perched on the young man's shoulder hurled a peanut, which hit her square on the nose.

Blind with misery, fear, and humiliation, Tracey sat down in an adjacent room. Behind a big closed door was a hideous caterwauling, as if animals were being systematically murdered. From another, slightly ajar, came a murmur of voices, one of them undoubtedly Dr. Baldwin's, but Tracey was too numb now to feel any desire but to escape.

In a few minutes a woman emerged, leading a Labrador, and a surprisingly small white-coated figure behind her motioned to Tracey to come into the office. "So you're Tracey?" A hand clasped hers in a quick, friendly grip. "Sit down, sit down —" A chair was shoved her way. "Glad you finally made it."

"I'm so embarrassed," Tracey choked. "We live way out beyond Silver Spring. I don't get downtown very often and I — took all the wrong buses."

Jane Baldwin leaned forward on her folded arms and smiled. "You poor child," she said, and instantly everything was all right. There was something about her voice, rich and soothing as velvet. Or maybe it was her eyes: they were like velvet too — big brown-velvet blossoms behind her glasses, with an expression that was both twinkling and wise. Or her smile! When she smiled it was as if a light bloomed behind her face. And you, who had been chilled and quaking, became warmly relaxed.

"Your aunt tells me you've always wanted to be a vet."

"Yes, from the time I was just a little kid." Tracey settled back with a grin. "By the time I was eight or nine my mother decided it would be a relief — at least there'd be somebody to take care of the animals I was continually dragging home!"

The doctor laughed. "I guess you realize what you're up against. It's a pretty tough row for a girl. Two years premed, then four years vet school before you can even take your state boards. It's no picnic, believe me, and the men do their best to keep you out."

"I've noticed that!"

"I guess you met Whitney? Whit, we call him. He's had three years at Maryland but had to drop out. He can teach you a lot."

29

Tracey's heart was beginning to pound. She held her breath as the doctor asked, "By the way, have you had any experience?"

"I worked last summer at a pet store in Silver Spring."

"Good. Can you give shots?"

"Well, no, I've never tried."

"Take temperatures?"

"Not even that. But I'll learn! I — I'll work my heart out for you, Dr. Baldwin."

"Gracious, I wouldn't want that — just a good all-around job. I may as well tell you I'd promised the place to the daughter of a friend of mine, but it turns out she has to go to summer school, though she may be back. If she does come later, I guess we can work things out. By the way, when could you start?"

"Next week," gasped Tracey. "School's out this Thursday. I — I could even start Saturday if you want!"

"Let's make it Monday, nine o'clock." The doctor stood up and held out her hand. "Better leave home early," she warned with a cheerful wink. "And this time carry a map!"

Tracey was so excited she tried to go through the wrong door, and the doctor had to grab her arm and steer her about. Her flushed face and shining eyes swept the waiting room where all the mere clients sat. Already she felt a little superior to them, one of the staff.

When the cocker sprang at her again, she paused to pat its head. And when the parrot screamed: "Cut that out! Gimme a kiss!" she too laughed. Her only disappointment was that *he* wasn't there to give her a final dirty look — that Whit.

Tracey thrived on conflicts. She had a sudden, eager, flashing desire to pit herself against him. Boy! Wouldn't he be surprised to learn she'd gotten the job!

30

Chapter 3

SHE MANAGED to get home without getting lost and, late as it was, stopped to feed Cricket and Littlebit. Liz lived in a brick ranch-style house with a large fenced yard just across the street from the apartment house. The dogs had already spent a lot of time there, so they felt at home. Also, Liz loved them like a sister, which was comforting.

Still, Tracey's heart hurt as they came bounding to meet her, jumping and clamoring for attention. "Wait, you kids! Take it easy," she scolded softly, squatting in the kitchen dishing out their food. "I surely do appreciate this, Mrs. Cadell," she said, looking up as Liz's mother came in from the garden.

"We don't mind, at least for a while," said the pleasant, heavy-set woman, putting down her garden shears. "Of course, we'll be going to the shore for the summer. Maybe we could leave the key or something."

"That'd be wonderful, if it's O.K. with Mr. Cadell. Say, where's Liz?"

"Out in back with some of the girls. Why don't you join them?"

"Think I will." Tracey sniffed appreciatively. "What're they cooking that smells so good?"

It proved to be hamburgers — with a barbecue sauce that Mitzy Miller was attempting to make in a battered pan on the grill while Liz read directions from a book. "You take these two cans of tomato paste, it says here, and then you grate some garlic and a big onion — "

"Go on, go on, next page, we've done all that."

31

"Help! Somebody else take over the onions — I'm weeping buckets!" Joan Hampton dramatically flung down her knife and wiped her eyes.

"Well, if anybody thinks I'm going to sully my sweet breath with garlic and onions when the guys are coming at eight — " said Kathy Carlson, and there was a general chorus of assent.

Too late, Tracey recognized the attractive crowd of girls. The Tri Chis, they called themselves. Liz's sorority, for Pete's sake, and here she'd come barging in!

Not that she wasn't roundly welcomed. Liz loyally saw to that. "Good! Here's Tracey to help us. Believe it or not, Tracey's an expert — she learned to cook from all those Government bulletins she's always sending for to learn about pigs and stuff."

"Well, if it's pigs she cooks for, count me out!" somebody cracked. And somebody else laughed, "Darling, there's not too much difference." And Liz ordered: "Pipe down, you-all, and be thankful a real chef showed up. Here, Trace! It's all yours — "

Protesting, Tracey found herself in charge of the scorching mess. She felt awful. Even remembering that Liz had begged her to join this group when it was organized in ninth grade didn't help much. She'd known even then that she'd never really belong. They thought her crazy, these kids. A freak. An adorable freak, maybe, but a freak, nonetheless. And she thought *them* a little crazy. Their hysterical laughter over things that didn't strike her funny at all. Their going into a frenzy over clothes, or some stupid singer who didn't cut his hair and sounded — honestly sounded to her like a dog in dire pain.

Or take the absolutely fantastic way they acted sometimes around boys. Putting on personalities that weren't theirs at all. Much as she thought of Liz, she was flabber-

32

gasted to see Liz, who was really quite down to earth and serious and had some simply wonderful thoughts about reforming the world — she had blushed to see this self-same Liz cavorting with somebody like Skip Morrow as if she didn't have a brain in her head.

It was all rather sad and puzzling. Tracey felt so awfully much older. Like a big sister or a teacher almost — somebody who ought to remonstrate with them. Yet it wasn't exactly like that, either. She had a forlorn knowledge that she'd like to be able to share their enthusiasms, step down to their level, behave as they did. But the few times she'd tried, she'd felt — and known she appeared — a fool. Worse, she'd felt a phony.

This she had tried vainly to point out to Mother. " Conform? How can I conform? " she'd cried in honest desperation. "I don't know how! And it's not convincing when I do. I've got to be honest, Mom. I've got to be me — myself! "

Curiously, she felt at home with boys. She sensed, and it furnished some small comfort, that lots of girls were terribly uneasy, and the absurd and incredible things they sometimes did were an attempt to deny that uneasiness. But boys were Tracey's best friends. Boys were a little like animals — awkward and rather pathetic in some ways, but steady and dependable and fundamentally very loving. Boys had always tagged her home from school and hung around the apartment and stayed for dinner, and asked her to go places with them.

The only reason she didn't accept more often, to the consternation of her mother and the continued amazement of the girls, was that she honestly could not find many boys to whom she could talk about things that interested her. And because whenever she did go someplace with a boy, they were bound to run into other couples and the

33

minute you and some boy you really liked and could enjoy teamed up with other couples you were sunk. The girls, with their bright, coquettish chatter, simply took over, stole the show, froze her out. What had started out to be something honest, gay, and good, was somehow ruined.

Tracey found herself doing most of the work now, flipping the hamburgers and salvaging the almost hopeless sauce by adding most of a bottle of catsup and some lemon juice.

"Hey, I didn't come here to slave," she announced. "All I came for was a handout." And fixing herself a bun, she retreated with it to sit by the steps and feed bites of it to the frantically begging dogs.

They didn't miss her. Except to yell, "Swell sauce, boss," they went on discussing the house party they were going to have at Liz's after school was out, settling on a date. There were a lot of conflicts. Some were going to camp, some on trips with their folks. And there were the boys to consider, the boys who'd be coming down. It sounded like fun, whenever they had it. Suddenly something stabbed Tracey — a totally unexpected and unreasonable desire to be invited. Even if she didn't belong.

Outsider. The word sneaked up, hit her with full impact. Nuts! This was silly. She'd always been outside and never really minded, had even been maybe a little bit proud of it. But somehow tonight with the voices so gay, and the smell of charcoal mingling with the sweetness of trampled grass and the roses that spilled over the fence — Tonight, with the sky turning from soft, breathless pink to twilight filled with secret excitements, and the first stars trembling through, it was lonely. She'd have given almost anything to be one of them.

A car tore up the drive, stopped with a honk and a

heralding roar. Male voices approached, and the scuff of sturdy male loafers. Good! Here came the boys. Yet, absurdly, Tracey's heart began to hammer. They streaked right past her, not seeing her there among the vines. All except Skip Morrow, who paused, turned on his heel.

"Well, hey, if it isn't Trace! How you doin', kid? Whadd'ya know for sure?"

Now a couple of others sauntered over. She felt how very much they liked her: there was something comradely about them, like brothers. Again she felt a pang of nostalgia for those long-lost days out West. She sensed something affectionate, almost applauding in the boys' attitude. "Hey! I hear you ran out on Old Man Scoggins this afternoon, and is he sore!"

"Is he?" Tracey asked in such absolute innocence that everybody laughed. "I had to," she explained. "I absolutely couldn't wait another minute. As it was, I was two hours late. But I got the job," she announced. "With Dr. Baldwin. I go to work next Monday."

"Not *the* Dr. Baldwin!" Skip exclaimed, and whistled. "Wow! The big cat-and-dog dame herself? Well, I'll be! Hey, kids! Here I've been scraping the barrel for a summer job for weeks, and Trace picks off one just like that. With Dr. Baldwin, no less."

"Tracey, you didn't!" Liz cried, and went on dumping paper plates into the trash. "Why, that's marvelous!"

A couple of other girls blinked and shrugged. One said, "Who's Dr. Baldwin?" And another, "What'll you have to do, Tracey?"

"Oh, be general flunky and scrubwoman at first, I suppose — clean kennels, exercise dogs, hold 'em for shots. But it's the best way to learn — being around a really fine doctor, especially a surgeon. I'm hoping to get to watch some operations. And while I don't wish any

35

animal hard luck, I hope there'll be at least one pyometra case. It's extremely interesting, and the percentage of recoveries is low."

Suddenly everybody was laughing, even the boys. Skip grabbed her, mid-sentence, hugged her and ruffed her already wild blond locks. "You're nuts! Know it? You're absotively nuts, and if I ever get a dog with piamet — whatever you call it — I promise I'll let you operate!"

He meant well — they all did. There was nothing mean about any of it. But her throat went tight; her chest hurt. "Well, I gotta beat it," she said. And picking Cricket and Littlebit up bodily, she carried them into the basement, where their beds were kept.

"'Night now," she said to them. "Be good! You hear?" And biting her lip, she went stamping back across the street.

It was still wonderful, almost too wonderful, this thing that had happened this afternoon. But nobody understood.

Chapter 4
_____

HE WAS SITTING at the desk that Monday morning when, taut with anticipation, Tracey arrived. She'd had the impression that Whitney was handsome before, but actually she'd been too scared to look. Now she saw that his curly hair was scaled down to a crisp bronze brush. His sandy brows were heavy and rather low, making a formidable bridge across his keen, short, extremely attractive nose. He had a square jaw, a strong, square face, and his eyes were absolutely the most luscious mahogany shade she'd ever seen outside a just-curried bay colt.

36

Tracey, in her intensity, stared. She never did anything by halves. And feeling this enthralled appraisal, even while trying to take down information and answer the phone, the young man jumped.

"Oh! So you got here!" He gave her a quick, startled, vaguely disgusted glance and jerked his head. "Go on back, ask Bert to give you an apron. I haven't got time for you till Mrs. Phillips gets here."

Mrs. Phillips was evidently the receptionist, and the office was already half full, with other patients streaming in. Tracey went bungling through the first door she saw — into the examining room. It seemed to be empty, so she pushed through a second — into bedlam. This room was immense, and in ranks and tiers of gray-steel kennels dogs leaped, barked, hurled themselves against their bars, and howled. The racket intensified, if possible, at sight of a stranger. Through wide doors in the rear, other dogs were being led back in from their morning exercise.

A small but firm little man in gray denim was having a rather hard time with a Great Dane who plainly didn't want to return. He was snarling and yanking at the end of the leash, while the kennel man quietly but steadily inched him toward his pen.

Not seeing anyone else to ask, Tracey approached, albeit keeping her distance. "I — I'm the new assistant. I wonder if you're Bert."

"No, Miss, I'm Jake. Bert's upstairs starting baths, but maybe I can help you."

The ominous rumbling in the Dane's throat became a roar. Suddenly, fangs bared, the huge dog lunged. In sheer reflex action, Tracey sprang backward, knocking over a bucket of sudsy disinfectant with a crash that added to the general hubbub, while the water went sloshing across the floor. Pale, shaking, she found herself cringing against the wall. " I — don't think he likes me! "

" Aw, Butch don't like nobody much. He's a bad actor. Hate to see him come to board every year. Now no more of that, you hear? " the kennel man ordered sternly, and somehow maneuvered the monster into his pen. He turned cheerfully back to Tracey. " Never show fear, Miss. Some people say animals can smell it. I doubt that. But they can sense it. Thing to do is talk in a tone that shows who's boss. Always be kind, but let 'em know you mean business." He reached for a mop.

At that moment, Dr. Baldwin herself came striding through, buttoning the sleeves of her starched white coat. " Good morning, Tracey. I see you made it. 'Morning, Jake."

" Oh, good morning, Dr. Baldwin! " Tracey gushed in a glory of relief. " I'm so glad to see you. I'm afraid I — "

The doctor wasn't listening. " Jake, I'll be in surgery all morning," she informed him in crisp, incisive tones. " When Whit has time, tell him to prepare Mrs. Cassidy and stand by; I may need him." Her trim little heels clicked up the open flight of metal steps.

Tracey stood crushed, cursing her own impetuosity. Fool! Fool! Why hadn't she had enough sense to realize that the busy doctor would have no time for her? She was also troubled: who was Mrs. Cassidy?

" Mrs. Cassidy's a chow," Jake chuckled at her expression. " We often call the dogs by their owners' names — saves confusion."

" Somebody come out, please! Somebody come out, please! " The call was coming from the loudspeaker on the wall over the intercommunication system.

" That's you they'll be wanting," Jake informed her. " Grab an apron from the supply room and get out there — they're probably short-handed."

Tracey dashed desperately in the direction he pointed. The only apron she saw was big and scratchy, designed for a person twice her size, and she didn't know how to tie it. Thus ludicrously tented and now painfully aware that some of the smelly disinfectant had slopped her skirt and thoroughly soaked one sandal, she made an earnest if squishing re-entrance.

All the chairs were filled, and Mrs. Phillips was busily taking down information on her little card. "Owner's name and address, please. The dog's name?" At the sight of Tracey she looked up, openmouthed. The ghost of a grin jerked Whitney's mouth too as he led a reluctant Labrador past her.

"Start bringing back the dogs to be boarded," he ordered.

"Back where?"

"To the kennel room —" He didn't actually say "stupid," but that's what his tone implied. "Tie them up out there."

Tracey approached the first dog, a beautiful beagle, obviously terrified, that kept trying to scramble onto its owner's lap. "Now, baby, come on — they won't hurt you. Now baby doll, be good," the owner wheedled. And Tracey managed to half lug, half drag him away.

Winning and influencing her own dogs was vastly different, it bleakly occurred to her, from influencing those of somebody else. She had a lot to learn. Still, most of them came peaceably The trouble was what to do with them when you got them into the chaotic kennel room. Most of the pens were full. You had to grab a rope and just tie them wherever you could. Everybody else was so busy that nobody paid any attention. There didn't seem to be another spot in sight when Tracey came trudging back with a particularly anxious, squirming dachshund.

"Take it easy now, Heidi! Take it easy." She stroked its satiny body and kept talking to it gently. There was a warm glow of excitement within her, despite the lingering edges of her own nervousness. She was actually here, a part of this important and thrilling institution — a new, small, insignificant part, but a part, nonetheless! And she'd learn. She'd keep her eyes and ears open and be a model of efficiency — lightning-quick, dependable, courteous, trustworthy, apt — Tracey strung her potential virtues like beads on a chain. Soon they'd recognize her value, and say of her, " A jewel, a perfect gem." And someday when she too was a renowned woman veterinarian clipping through her own hospital in a white coat, Dr. Baldwin herself would proudly reflect: "I trained her. She was just a green kid when she came to me, but I saw definite promise. I saw she had a lot on the ball — "

"Hey, you — the new girl! Come here! " That could be but one voice, thrilling and imperious.

Hastily she tied a rope to the dog's collar and settled for an unoccupied corner, where it could be fastened to a table leg. "Hold still now! Hold still," she pleaded, for the slippery little rascal kept trying to dive between her legs.

Then she darted dutifully to answer the summons from the examining room.

" Oh, what a beautiful thing! " she exclaimed. For Whit had a gorgeous collie on the table; obviously it didn't want to take the shot he was preparing to give.

" Hold him. Be still and hold him, for Pete's sake."

Tracey grabbed the hind quarters, clean and silky, while Whitney pinched the proper fold of skin up near the neck. She watched, fascinated, as with one swift jab he plunged the needle in.

" There now, that didn't hurt, did it, Jenkins? " He spoke

40

amiably to the dog and made little nuzzling motions with his nose as he briskly massaged the skin. "All that fuss! Aren't you ashamed?" His face was — different, when he was talking to the dog. It was relaxed and amused and full of tenderness, And the pointed nose went up in response, sniffed back at him, and the collie attempted to lick his face.

Then suddenly all was pandemonium. "Get the ropes! Watch out! Shut the doors!" Everybody seemed to be yelling at once — from the reception room on one side and the kennel room on the other. "Where'd it go? There it is. Catch it! Catch it!"

In one swift motion, Whitney had the big dog off the table and safely back to wherever he'd come from. "Well, what're you waiting for?" he hollered as Tracey stood gaping. "Get busy! Get going!"

"Going where? For — for what?"

"The dachs. A dachs got loose!"

Bewildered, Tracey rushed out front, where most of the commotion seemed to be centered. People were clustered around the front door, and a few clients had gone outside and were helpfully looking up and down the street. Mrs. Phillips returned from the sidewalk herself in a minute, looking disheveled and very much concerned.

"Well, we've simply got to find it, that's all," she declared, snatching up the phone. "I'll call the owner right away to report, in case it should somehow get back home."

Whit ran back to round up all possible help — Jake, the head kennel man, and Zabrinski, who did the clipping, and Bert, who was in charge of baths, and a couple of others. Young as he was, there was something very authoritative and compelling about Dr. Baldwin's assistant, and the others fanned out according to his directions.

41

"You, Tracey," he ordered, "go on across the street. Cover this end of the park."

"Y-Yes, Sir!" Still in the ill-fitting apron, she tore off, shocked and troubled. What a dreadful thing to have happen! Just too awful for everybody involved. She wondered what Dr. Baldwin would say when she heard. And how in the world did you ever explain a mishap like that to the owner?

It was a glorious summer day. The grass was wet in Rock Creek Park. Sunlight came cascading down through the tall, soaring trees, making even their shadows sparkle. Birds went dipping and singing, and clopping merrily along the bridle path came a group of girls from a neighboring riding academy, all looking so pert, so carefree, that Tracey couldn't help the pang that smote her. Her feet were soaked. She felt foolish trudging futilely and frantically about calling, "Here, doggy! Here, doggy!" and whistling.

The girls looked at her in amazement. She could hear their murmured comments and their laughter spilling back. She was suddenly aware of the spectacle she must present in the apron. And though she usually didn't care how she looked — was, in fact, vaguely aware that her very uniqueness had a certain appeal — this was different. Something hot went stinging through her. She felt conspicuous and absurd.

Turning her back, she stamped earnestly on, averting her eyes from the cars that went zooming along the drive. But a long blue station wagon slowed down and honked. An attractive young blond woman with her hair in a bright bandanna, leaned out. "Aren't you from Dr. Baldwin's?" Looking troubled but friendly, she opened the door. "We can't have the entire hospital stopped because of Heidi. Get in. I'll take you back."

42

"Is it your dog?" Tracey blunderingly consoled. "I'm so sorry. I know you must feel just awful."

"Well, yes, Heidi's a valuable dog. She's been grand champion in her class, won a lot of trophies, and we were planning to retire her for breeding. What's more, she's a lovable little thing. But we'll find her, I feel sure. And these things happen. I'm not blaming you, dear, and I'm sure Dr. Baldwin won't either."

"Blame — me?" Tracey gasped. She jerked upright as the truth struck her a hideous, walloping blast.

Both she and Whit had been hauling dogs back, and there'd been a couple of dachshunds. But this one — this was the slippery character called Heidi! The one she'd had to fasten to the table. Oh, why hadn't she made sure it couldn't wriggle free? taken every precaution? This was all her fault!

Tracey was too stunned and heartsick to answer. They drove through the park a while longer, Tracey wishing desperately for the sight of a small bronze, low-slung body. Then Mrs. Frederick parked, and the fervent new would-be wonder girl of the Baldwin Animal Hospital slunk back inside in disgrace.

The others had also returned by now and were busy at their tasks. To Tracey's surprise, nobody scolded her for this ghastly mishap. The doctor herself had come downstairs and was slipping into a fresh coat before beginning the eleven o'clock office hours. She grinned faintly at sight of her new employee. "Where in the world did you get that apron? Go back in the supply room and try to find something that fits. And while you're there get a rubber apron too. Bert said something about needing you upstairs with baths."

"Dr. Baldwin, I feel just terrible. I — I can't tell you how — "

43

"Don't try. Skip it. These things can't be helped."

The rubber apron was long and awkward and smelled funny. And when she was hurrying through the kennel room the Great Dane spotted her and hurled himself so fiercely against the bars and barked so savagely that she had a sharp impulse to run. She was a failure already: everybody knew it now, even the dogs!

Bert was working on a poodle, and two more awaited his attention. "You Tracey? I'm Bert," he said bluntly, " and this here's Peppi, and he don't want a bath, d'you, Bud?" Bert was a big iron-jawed man with a bald head and huge red hands. He was unlettered and had a voice to wake the dead, but Tracey felt secure with him. Not awed, as with Dr. Baldwin. Or challenged, put to some grim, exciting test, as with Whit. But somehow befriended.

"Hold still, Peppi," she said, approaching the bath table and holding the threshing body as Bert began to wash out the eyes and nostrils. "This is going to make you feel good."

She was slopped and messy again by noon. There were hairs down her back from the clipping table; she itched. Tired and dispirited, she washed up before going into the small but comfortable lounge upstairs to eat her lunch. She sat down self-consciously on the studio couch and unwrapped her sandwiches. The cold boiled ham tasted flat; the hardboiled egg stuck in her throat. She thought of Liz and the gang, who were probably out shopping for beach clothes, picking out cute new bathing suits and shorts and halters, and then going to a Hot Shoppe for lunch. She brooded on the tantalizing picture — Well, but this was what she *wanted*, wasn't it? Only why was she driven to want it so much?

Or take those girls in the park this morning, cantering so blithely along. A deeper envy struck. Why couldn't she

44

afford riding lessons too? She used to save her allowance to go riding, only the rates had gone up so much, and with college to consider — Well, she'd have her own horse someday — horses — her own farm, raise blooded stock. Go back to Wyoming, that was it, and buy the Carter ranch! After she'd been in practice enough years to make enough money — it would take tons. It would take — forever, she realized bleakly. When you considered college and then vet school and interning with some other doctor probably before you could even consider going out on your own —

"How'd you like a cup of coffee?" Whit stood before her holding a steaming percolator and a plastic cup.

"Oh — oh, yes, please!" She'd imagined she'd smelled coffee from the direction of the little kitchen where diets were prepared. But for anyone, especially this forbidding man, to offer her some, was almost too much to expect. For a second she wanted to weep.

Wordlessly, Tracey drank it. It was black as a Labrador's coat. But it revived her. By the time Mrs. Phillips came tripping up and beckoned to her, she felt as if there might be some hope for her yet.

"I'm going to lunch in a few minutes, Tracey, and Doctor says you can take over the desk. Come down, I'll show you, and if you have any problems just ask one of the boys."

It wasn't hard. Anybody with good sense could do it, especially at this hour of the day when things had quieted down a bit. The burden of the lost dachshund still weighed heavily on her heart, however. Where was it wandering, poor little thing? By now it might have been struck by a car, be lying stricken in some ditch.

But, no, she didn't dare brood on that. The thing now was to keep her mind on the business at hand. The fact

that they'd trusted her with this responsibility was, like
the coffee, reinvigorating. If only she could get people's
names straight now and not let anything else disastrous
happen!

The morning, for all its hectic aspects, had seemed to
last forever. The afternoon went faster, probably because
it was more interesting. Whit took her under his wing. He
was still gruff and cryptic, but patient, probably because
she was so obviously stricken over the mishap of the
morning. He introduced her to all the animals and their
ailments and showed her how the charts were kept.

"All charts are supposed to be filled out and every dog
thoroughly checked by noon. Of course today's different
— we're running behind schedule."

"I know," she said, and bit her lip.

He didn't reply. He, like everybody else, seemed to be
sedulously avoiding the subject. It was almost worse than
if somebody'd given her a stiff bawling out and gotten it
over with.

"We try to take care of all the skin cases in the afternoon. They take quite a while, and if you're in the midst
of a treatment, it's hard to stop. The dogs are exercised
again at four. You can help with that."

Tracey blanched. "Not that Great Dane, I hope," she
blurted. "He acts as if he'd like to tear me limb from
limb."

"You aren't the only one!"

"Don't tell me you're scared of him too!" she dared,
giving him a sly look.

"You bet your sweet life I'm scared of him. Jake's the
only one who can handle that beast, and the rest of us
let him. Of course you know you're never supposed to
show fear, no matter what."

46

"Poor things. Most of 'em look too miserable to scare anybody." Tracey paused beside the cage of a wirehaired fox terrier that was just beginning to revive from its morning's anesthetic. Still dazed and unaware of what had happened to it, it raised its head and howled. "Poor boy. It's all right. Don't worry —"

"Of course you can't afford to go around getting sentimental, either." Whit said bluntly. "You haven't got time to baby them. Not if you do the job that's expected of you."

And he was right, Tracey thought quickly and humbly. A girl who'd been so incredibly careless as to let a valuable dog escape was in no position to stand around mooning.

She was supposed to get off at four thirty, but it was after five before she left. An emergency came in at the last minute — a dog that had been hit by a car. For a few sickening seconds Tracey thought it might be the dachs. But the small patient that Dr. Baldwin lifted so gently onto the table was a mixed breed.

"Both hind legs are broken and there's an internal rupture, I'm afraid. Take him up to surgery, boys. I'll have to operate."

Tracey's heart began to beat double time. Before she knew it, she had grabbed Whit's arm. "Do — d' you suppose I could watch?"

"Are you crazy?" He whirled to her, glowering and aghast. "Mop up the mess and go home!"

Tired, mad, and miserable, still scratchy with hairs and smelling to high heaven, Tracey dragged herself into the apartment. She was surprised to find that Gammy had set the table in the dining L instead of the breakfast nook and was using candles. Mother, looking cool in a linen sunback after work, was arranging some roses. And

47

Dudley, all dressed up in clean slacks and a shirt of seven different shades of pink, had his feet on the coffee table, discussing genetics with Aunt Azalea.

"Surprise, surprise!" Trailing beads, charm bracelets, ruffles, and the knitting she carried everywhere, Aunt Azalea pattered across the room. Tracey was nearly stabbed with a knitting needle as she was clutched in a fragrant embrace. "A little party, darling, in honor of your first day. How did it go?" she asked, beginning to knit furiously as she rattled on. "I told Dr. Baldwin, 'You'll be lucky to get that girl!' Those were my exact words. 'She's one in a million,' I told her, and now she knows. She'll be calling me up to thank me, I predict, within the hour —"

"Yes, dear, how was it?" Her mother turned interestedly from the table. "Tell us all about it. How did it go?"

" How did it go?" Tracey stood dumbly facing them, not knowing whether to laugh or cry. "I lost a valuable dog, that's all. I hadn't been there half an hour before it got away and hasn't been heard from since!"

"Now, dear, now, dear," they were all saying. "It could happen to anybody."

"I know," she wailed. "I know — but it happened to *me!*"

Chapter 5

THE FIRST DAY is always the worst day on any job. Things get a little better on the second. And by the end of the second week Tracey was bouncing into the hospital feeling as if she had personally founded the institution and was running it single-handed.

She helped lead the dogs out for exercising, and while they were absent helped scrub and sterilize the pens. With Whit she would check the animals. He taught her how to take temperatures of the sick ones and, under his supervision, prepare the special diets. He was still curt with her clumsiness, and annoyed by her obvious and flagrant desire to please.

"Relax, will you?" he often barked. "You make me nervous flashing around here like some canine Florence Nightingale."

He even took to calling her Florrie, not realizing that it gave her a perverse, ecstatic thrill. A special name for her, even one meant to be satiric! That proved that she had impressed him, didn't it? Oh, how wonderful just to be near him! To jump at his roaring summons, to drop whatever she was doing to scurry to his side, to serve him with humble zeal!

She felt like a puppy herself in this new, delicious role. She longed to act like a puppy! To hurl herself at him, yipping with pleasure at their reunion each morning! To snatch up little offerings in her teeth and come trotting to him with them. But the best she could do was bring him a book from her library. Or once a cherry pie on which she'd lavished two hours of her attention.

At the last minute, though, she got self-conscious and blushed furiously and explained that the pie was made from a recipe that had won a prize in a national bake-off contest, and she'd thought it would be nice to try. She'd brought it down for all the "help," only would he mind cutting and sampling it first?

Whit stared at her in glowering astonishment. Then very gravely he put down the thermometer he'd just been reading and went back to wash his hands. "I'm honored," he claimed, returning. "Why, Florrie, if you hadn't put it like that I'd almost say you were trying to ply me with cooking!"

"If that's a pun it stinks," she retorted. "All I'd like to ply you with right now is a pair of surgical scissors. Over the head!" she added. And snatching the pie from which he'd just gouged a sizable chunk, she stalked off with it.

The nerve of him, seeing through her devices like that, and what's more, taunting her with them! The intolerable gall!

She was too upset to be very gracious, passing the pie around among Jake and Zabrinski and Bert and the rest. And when they insisted she save a piece for herself, she slipped downstairs and headed for the pen where Butch, the Great Dane, was pacing.

"Hi, Butch," she said softly, crouching. "You still mad? You still hate everybody?" She inched forward, and holding a scrap of the pie in her fingers, pushed it in. "Here. Don't tell anybody, but I brought you something."

Butch snarled, and Tracey backed hastily off. But there was a glad excitement in her breast as the dog snuffed at the pie. In one snap he wolfed it down and stood quivering, the huge black face fixed in a glaring challenge, as if daring her to offer more.

50

"O.K., O.K., here y'are." She thrust more scraps in, all the while visiting gently. "You uncomfortable in there, huh? You lonesome? You wanta get out and run? Well, I don't blame you, a big fellow like you cooped up most of the summer. I wouldn't do it to you," she traitorously told him. "Boy! If I had a dog like you and was going away, I'd sure take you along."

"Tracey, what in the world are you doing?"

Startled, Tracey sprang to her feet. She hadn't heard Dr. Baldwin approaching. "Don't you know there are rules against feeding the animals between meals?"

"Yes, Ma'am." Tracey stood at rigid attention. "I'm very sorry."

"What were you giving him, anyhow?"

"Pie, Dr. Baldwin. Some — cherry pie."

"Pie!" the doctor cried in amazement. "Where'd you get it?"

"It's some I baked at home," she blurted out. "I — thought I'd bring it in for the staff."

"Well, I didn't get any. I work here too, you know. Where's mine?"

Tracey gasped. The voice was so amiable — and reasonable. She felt dreadfully embarrassed. "Oh, I'm sorry! If I'd thought — well — that you wanted some —"

The doctor laughed. "Relax, Tracey, relax," she said, almost as Whit had done. "I'm not sacrosanct," She turned to Butch, and to Tracey's vast admiration, reached in and roughed the great head. "Was it good, Butch, huh? Did you like it?" She winked at Tracey. "I guess a little cherry pie never hurt a dog, even Butch."

"I'm trying to win his friendship," Tracey confessed. "He scared me so that first day that I thought maybe if I could win him around —"

"Ah, Butch wouldn't hurt anybody, would you?" The

51

doctor's confident hands continued to caress the panting, almost piteously grateful dog. "Like some people," she commented dryly, and her dark eyes twinkled, "his bark's a lot worse than his bite."

Like Whit! Tracey realized gratefully, and wanted to laugh. How much alike they were — the big wonderful, terrifying dog, and the big wonderful, terrifying man. She felt newly driven to win and master both of them.

Tracey tucked in her emotional shirttails; Tracey rolled up her sleeves. Before this summer's over, she resolved, I'll have them both eating out of my hand!

Endearing though the incident was, Tracey still found it difficult to overcome her awe of Jane Baldwin. She was so — terrific. So simply terrific in her calm, steady, friendly yet authoritative administration of the hospital! Nothing fazed her, from the most unreasonable customer to the most unreasonable pet.

Tracey watched her in action with both, and marveled. She seemed to have a little switchboard of personalities that she could plug in at a touch and fit to every occasion. You could somehow feel her hovering in the background looking the situation over as the receptionist took down the information. Then when she came to grips with the client she would know exactly how to proceed.

Most of the owners were well-to-do. They came largely from the mansions or artistically restored Early American row houses of exclusive old Georgetown. Many were high-ranking Government officials or members of the diplomatic set. But there were many everyday people too — Government workers, clerks, and an occasional earnest child clutching a purse full of pennies in one hand and a forlorn-looking mutt in the other.

Whoever they were, Dr. Baldwin was able to speak their language, reflect their special outlook, meet their special needs. And yet throughout, whether gravely advising the wife of an ambassador that she didn't think Griselda, a beautiful Kerry blue, would be better off wearing boots and a raincape, or chatting with an urchin who absolutely insisted on seeing her, and her personally, about his cat, she managed, this amazing woman, to remain serenely and gloriously her fundamental self.

Oh, to be able to emulate such a woman! To get over being so impetuous, so intense, about everything; to have that much control!

When it came to the four-footed patients, Tracey marveled at the doctor's stamina, her wisdom, her sheer, undaunted strength. She saw her pick Butch himself up one day and throw him bodily onto the table. "He's been extra cross lately. I'm afraid he's not feeling well and I want to give him a thorough going over. Here, Tracey, you can help."

"Who, me?" Tracey gulped.

"Yes, you." The doctor's lip quirked. "I thought you two were getting to be such friends."

Hoping desperately not to fall flat on her already shaky reputation, Tracey took hold of the sleek but massive limbs. A sense of wonder flowed through her. What a glorious beast he was! And how trusting, under the doctor's expertly probing fingers, how almost pathetically subdued! Or maybe — the strange, almost presumptuous idea occurred to Tracey — maybe he felt safe with her as well. Maybe Butch, the bad boy, found some slight comfort and security in her own young, hopeful touch.

"The abdomen seems tender. I'm afraid he may have an intestinal infection. I'm going to prescribe an antibiotic and put him on a special diet. I'll make it out and I want you and nobody else to cook it and feed him for a while."

Tracey caught her breath. Dr. Baldwin, she suspected, was taking advantage of the situation to help Tracey's personal campaign to win and influence Butch.

"What, no cherry pie?" Tracey couldn't resist.

The doctor gave her a sidelong glance and laughed. "No. No cherry pie."

All this did not cancel the fact, however, that the dachshund was still missing. Tracey was half sick with guilt and concern every time she thought of it. She felt embarrassed and terribly troubled every time the subject came up. And although nobody made a point of talking about it, it did come up. Ads were run in *The Star*, *The Post*, and *The Georgetowner*. The pound was notified to watch. And Mrs. Frederick, the owner, still very gracious and understanding, but naturally concerned, came in occasionally to check.

Finally, unable to bear it any longer, Tracey bearded the doctor in her office one afternoon. "Dr. Baldwin, this has been worrying me so much I've just got to spill it," she said inelegantly. "How much would you say that missing dachshund is worth?"

The doctor considered, "Well, it's hard to estimate. Mrs. Frederick told me she paid only two hundred for it, but it's won a lot of ribbons, and they'd planned to use it for breeding stock. Several thousand, I suppose, in the long run."

Tracey's face fell. Before these appalling figures her own plan was absurd.

"Why?" the doctor asked. "See here, Tracey, there's nothing you can do about it, and no reason why you should."

54

"But it's all my fault!" It was a relief to blurt it out at last. "I let him get away and everybody knows I did. That's what hurts — everybody's so nice and yet everybody knows whose fault it was! I was thinking — I know it sounds silly, but if you'd just hold out half my pay each week. I'd say take all, but there are expenses, and I've got to save a little something toward college. But I'd feel better — I'd honestly feel better — if you would."

"Tracey Temple —" The doctor shoved back in her chair and came around the desk to give her grieving assistant a little shake. "Listen, Tracey Temple, it was an accident. A serious accident, sure — let's not minimize that. But there's a vast difference between an accident and a crime. If I ever caught anybody mistreating an animal in my care, or welshing on the job, or failing to keep this place so clean we could invite the President to lunch — Well, in my book that'd be little short of a crime. But nobody with any sense of justice points the finger of blame or expects a sacrifice like that for something that couldn't be helped. Besides, we're insured for this sort of thing."

Tracey drew a deep breath of relief. It was silly, but her throat was full. She had to whirl and dart away before she made a complete idiot of herself.

Whit sauntered up behind her where she stood eagerly mixing and messing away at the small electric stove. "What're you cooking, Florence N? Another pie?"

"Sure. Don't you wish you had some?" Tracey set the pan down fast beside the sink for fear she'd drop it. She'd gone all limp inside.

"Brother! Does that smell awful! Who's the lucky dog?"

"Butch. He's on a special diet. Now, no remarks — to a dog with a stomach-ache this batch of i/d mixed with

55

his medicine and the raw beef I've been cooking ought to taste very good."

"All I can say is I'm glad you're the one to offer him this delectable little snack."

"So am I," Tracey acknowledged. "Butch and I are almost beginning to get along."

"Well, goody for your side!" Whit jeered lightly, and Tracey wondered why, oh, why she had to be so crazy about such a sarcastic man!

"You're still scared to death of him, aren't you?" she found herself crowing over him in sheer defense.

"My dear little Florrie, must you be so blunt? I simply admit the fact that he detests me, and I return the compliment. There's something very ugly and unlovable about that brute."

"There is not. He's just — lonesome. And he's sick. Poor thing! Maybe the reason he's sick is that he's so lonesome!"

"Could be," Whit said tartly and shrugged. "Could be, at that."

Tracey's heels clicked anxiously down the open steel steps. Butch had spurned her tastiest offerings for two days now. If only he would eat this! If only he would buck up and be happy enough — yes, ornery enough! — to eat. Not just lie there, disconsolate, glaring out at his captors, who wanted, oh, so much, to be friends.

She crouched, slipped the dish through the feeding slot. "Here y'are, boy. It's not cherry pie, but it's delicious, and I made it just for you."

Butch's response was a growl, followed by a savage barking. Well, good. While not exactly cordial, at least it proved he wasn't too completely sunk. "Atta boy, Butch! I don't expect you to thank me — just eat, boy, eat!"

She sprang up at the familiar call on the loud-speaker from out front. "Come out, please! Somebody come out and take away this ocelot! "

Ocelot? Tracey had barely time to grasp the word. Was somebody kidding? Instantly and quite overwhelmingly, she hoped not.

She went banging through doors and burst into the reception room. And there, sure enough, a man was pulling out of a regulation cat carrier a very small, very droopy, very sick ocelot.

" I just asked what was the cat's name and how old," Mrs. Phillips explained to Tracey, " when he said, ' This isn't a cat — it's an ocelot '! "

" But it *is* an ocelot," the tall, grim-jawed, distinguished-looking man insisted. " And this is Dr. Baldwin's Small Animal Hospital, isn't it? I want to see Dr. Baldwin about my sick ocelot! "

Tracey was shaking all over with excitement she was so amazed and pleased. If there was one thing she loved to a passion next to horses and ranches, it was zoo animals. Well, well, to think it really was a real, live if very sick ocelot!

" Dr. Baldwin is in surgery right now," she said with composure that surprised even her. " I'm sure she'll be glad to help you, though. Would you care to wait? "

" Wait! " exclaimed Mrs. Phillips, making frantic grimaces and waving her hands to signal the situation to Tracey, who had not, until this moment, taken into account an office full of other clients frozen to their chairs clutching their own pets. " Not in here, not here — maybe someplace in the back! "

" Well, no, not here, of course," Tracey said smoothly, and held out her arms. " Let me have him, will you? Oh, the poor little guy! " It was as natural as breathing, holding the limp bundle of spotted fur in her arms. He was like Ornrietta, only better, because there was more of him. He was like a baby. "What's his name?"

"Harry," said the gentleman, obviously relieved. "He's only eight months old and he seems to have come down with something. I've had him a couple of weeks and I do feel so bad. He's supposed to be a homecoming present for my wife, who's abroad. I wanted to surprise her."

"Well," said Tracey, "she should be surprised all right!"

"Look, I'm in a hurry. I have an appointment at the State Department." The man fished in his pockets. "Here's my card. I'd be so grateful if you'd just take care of Harry, and have the doctor call me at this number when she's free."

"I'd be glad to," said Tracey. And still cradling the beast, she carried him into the examining room.

Whit, who was busy in the adjoining pharmacy, jumped. "For Pete's sake!" he gasped. "What're you doing with that thing?"

"Don't be scared," she baited him. "Harry won't hurt you — he's only a poor little old sick baby ocelot."

"All right, all right, I get it," he snapped, "so lay off."

"I'm sorry," she said. Sorry? She was stricken! Why, oh, why did she have to go to such extremes, either bow down so utterly before him, or snatch opportunities like this to make him sore? It was all too confusing, too complex. Boys, most boys, were just — well, boys — easy to handle, to understand, to accept. But of course Whit was older, and he'd been to college all those years. He was, she realized in a dim, aching wonder, the first male person, unless you counted Jeff Carter, back on the ranch, she had ever really loved.

"Well, put that beast in a kennel and get out here and help me, will you? We're running late."

"Sure. Right away." Regretfully she deposited the

58

ocelot, latched the cage door. It lay there looking so helpless and wretched her heart ached. Sick animals were the most pitiful sight. You could never know how much they actually suffered; they couldn't even tell you where they hurt. They could only lie there, crouched in the protective shelter of their own limbs. And so often there was no way to reach them, no way to help.

"Tracey, come here. I need you!"

"Yes Sir! Right away, Sir!" Abandoning the little creature, Tracey flew to do Whit's bidding once more.

Dr. Baldwin diagnosed the ocelot's malady as enteritis. "I'm going to give him shots of chloromycetin and I hope we can pull him through. You know whom he belongs to, don't you?" she asked Tracey.

"Well, I — in all the excitement I didn't read the card."

"Just a five-star general, that's all. General George Fielding Heath. Knowing his wife as I do, I doubt if she'll be overjoyed if we succeed. You can hardly blame her, but we've got to try. Incidentally, I want to commend you on how you handled the whole situation."

A glow began to burn in Tracey's breast. It spread in warming trickles through her whole being. It was all right then. In spite of the dachshund episode she was of some value. "Who told you?" she asked, in the faint hope that despite his brusque reaction, Whit might have been sufficiently impressed.

"Mrs. Phillips." The doctor prepared the shot and gave it, and the limp little creature didn't even protest. "When I called the general he said the little thing hadn't eaten in three days. It'll die for sure if we don't get some nourishment into it." She looked up as Tracey stood hovering and anxious. The tips of her lips quirked. "Tracey, you're practically begging. Down, girl, down!"

59

"Butch is doing all right," Tracey pointed out. "Butch is snapping out of it, and I do mean snapping."

The doctor laughed. "O.K., then. I was going to ask you anyway I assure you nobody else is competing for the job. Here." She handed the sad small creature over. "Make it eggnog, and you'll probably have to spoon-feed it — an eye dropper would take too long. Keep trying every few hours."

Tracey loved it, how she loved it! To cuddle it against her breast and try to get a few dribbles of food into its disinterested, whiskery mouth. "Now, Harry, now, baby, be a good fellow," she kept crooning to it. Tipping its head back, she pulled the lip down and poured liquid into the space between the tightly clamped teeth, but it spilled when the creature turned miserably aside.

"Harry, poor little Harry, don't you know you'll die if you don't eat?" The prospect hurt. "Eat for Harry now, not for me." Patiently she worked the spoon in, pressing it toward the back of his jaws where he was forced to chew on it a little, and in sheer reflex, to swallow. "Good for you, Harry," she rejoiced. "Now some more —"

She knew that some of the fellows, passing where she sat with her charge, tapped their heads. She knew they thought she was a little nuts, as the kids at school always had. But here it didn't matter, because they were all a little nuts themselves. She guessed you had to be to love animals so much that your entire concept of bliss was to be surrounded by them. Well, not quite your *entire* concept, her heart amended. Her only true paradise would have to include an impossible guy called Whit.

Her persistence paid. It took an awful lot of spilled eggnog, but Harry began to get some of it inside. Gradually his strength returned, and with it his appetite. To her delight, Harry began to lick his own chops, the bowl, and even her fingers.

"You'd better watch out for him now," Jake warned, pausing to watch them one day. Harry was so much better he was practically frolicking. "That cat gets well he may decide he wants raw meat."

"Ah, Harry wouldn't touch a morsel of me, would you, Harry?" She poked a finger in his mouth to prove it, and the ocelot's pointed teeth opened and closed on it in those gentle bitings that are for any creature a form of caress. "Oh, how I'd love to have him!"

She had, in fact, nursed extravagant dreams: The general's wife might not want him. They might say, "In view of the selfless care that Harry's had from this devoted girl it seems only fitting that she take him." And she'd say, "Oh, my goodness, I hardly feel right about it, but you know, of course, that he'd be getting an excellent home."

Excellent home! The dream came crashing down. When domesticated animals like Cricket and Littlebit and Ornrietta had been humiliatingly kicked out. She brooded briefly on her own intensifying problem. Mr. Cadell had not, it seemed, really relished having enlarged his family by two dogs in the first place. And now that the rest of them were leaving for the shore, he had told Liz to tell Tracey they'd have to go.

A fang in her finger yanked Tracey back to the present. "Why, you ungrateful wretch!" Snatching it out, she gave Harry a brisk slap.

"See?" Jake triumphed. "Don't pay to take chances. Wild beasts is wild beasts and they can't really never be tamed."

"Yes, they can. There are hundreds of examples — ask any trainer."

"I said tamed, not trained. Y'ever read *Circus Doctor*? Guy that wrote that was a vet for Ringling Brothers, and he says the same thing. No siree, you can't change nature, Tracey — you just can't."

Tracey was annoyed. How silly could you get? The very idea of that small padding cat attacking — how absurd! Yet she had respect for Jake's opinion, if only because he'd worked with Dr. Baldwin so long.

"All I can say is I'm hurt," she told Jake exaggeratedly. "If I thought that ocelot didn't like me, after all I've done for him!"

"Wouldn't be he didn't like you, Tracey. Good gravy! Who could help liking a frisky, fine-looking girl like you?"

Tracey laughed, warmed by the honest admiration of this rough man. He wasn't Whit, but you couldn't have everything. "Thanks, Jake, but it seems to be my fate. Look at Butch — how I finally got him to eat and how he stills acts as if all he wants is a chance to get at me!"

"All he wants is a chance to love you," Jake said simply. And as she looked astonished, he added: "Just sashay up to his cage someday and pet him, the way Doctor does. And after you've petted him a few times so's he's used to the feel of it, why one of these days I'll let you take him out to the exercise run."

"Don't be in any hurry." Tracey protested doubtfully. But a great hope came bounding up in her heart. If she could finally begin to make real strides with Butch, anything was possible.

Practically anything!

Chapter 6

To cap the climax of those first two hectic, sometimes discouraging, exhausting, and wonderfully stimulating weeks, Dr. Baldwin summoned Tracey into the office one day.

"How'd you like to run a little errand to Union Station for me? To pick up a French poodle. A woman from Florida is passing through on her way to New York. She wants to board him with us for a few days."

"But a French poodle's a valuable dog!" Tracey protested.

"Why, sure! What about it?"

"You mean you'd trust me? You'd actually let me go?"

"Oh, for goodness' sake. You still thinking about that dachs? Of course I trust you, Tracey, or I wouldn't ask." The doctor opened her desk drawer. "Here's your cab fare and directions. If he gives you any trouble, just pick him up and carry him out. Now get out of that messy apron and scram."

Tracey scrammed. She didn't know when she'd been so excited, or so anxious to succeed.

She got out of the apron and vigorously scrubbed her arms, face, neck, and ears. Energetically, if futilely, she also tried washing at least the tag ends of her hair. Earlier she'd been interrupted while doing a mange case. And the dog, liberally sloshed with dark-brown medicine, had considerately awaited her return to give himself a violent shake.

The solution seemed to have a stubborn affection for her hair: it clung, leaving a sort of speckled-hen effect. Well,

63

but with all the crazy things people were doing to their hair these days, she reasoned — bleaching streaks out, dabbing streaks on — she might look right in style.

The smell, however, was something else. A potent aura of antiseptic and dog lingered, which she tried to drown in a liberal drenching of Midnight Madness perfume. She'd never been much of a perfume user before starting this job. Of course, the pet store had also had its smell problem. But somehow Dudley had not been the same incentive to keep from smelling too awful as His Highness, Mr. Whitney. Not, she realized, that either boy probably noticed, since they both worked with animals too. But if Dr. Baldwin could keep dainty no matter what, at least she could try.

You could do little about the dog hairs down your back without a shower. But a definite nip here and there informed Tracey she'd picked up a flea or two. Fleas were rare: Dr. Baldwin was such a demon about cleanliness that the poor fleas didn't stand a chance. Still, new crops did come in with new cases. Tracey slapped at herself, and gave her legs a quick squirt of bug kill. This odor, joining the medley of perfume, dog and mange medicine, didn't help any, but it would probably whisk away once she got outdoors.

Now scrubbed and shining, feeling trim and efficient in her white shirt with the stand-up collar and her full, swinging skirt with its broad leather belt, she dashed forth to fetch the poodle. Poodles were her favorite dog next to setters, preferably Irish, which she loved beyond all reason, probably because she'd had one on the ranch. Poodles were intelligent, keen, sensitive, if highstrung and at times a little stubborn. Oh, poodles could be prima donnas all right, and she only hoped this one took to her.

One thing more Tracey hoped as, enjoying the career-girl sensation it gave her, she stood on the curb flagging down a cab. She just hoped this dog had what she considered a civilized cut. Poodles were so beautiful with all that lovely, naturally curly hair! With the several clips there were to choose from, it seemed a crime, or at least a crying pity, to send dogs out onto the street with pompons on their tails and pantaloons on their legs, and the rest of their bodies shaved till they looked positively nude.

"The idea of doing this to a helpless creature who doesn't even know how silly he looks!" she'd fumed to Bert. "And who if he did, couldn't even complain!"

Bert had laughed. "Well, takes all kinds of dogs to please all kinds of people. Dogs reflect their owners' tastes. Show me a dog, and I'll tell you sight unseen what his owner's like, and I bet you could too."

Rocking toward the station on the slippery leather seat of the cab, Tracey studied her directions. As she paid the driver, she saw by her watch that the Golden Arrow was just about due. It was to stay in the station approximately fifteen minutes. She was to meet the woman, Mrs. Geraldine Vaughn, beside the car named the *Palisades*. Mrs. Geraldine Vaughn would by that time have repossessed Pierrot from the baggage car, and the transfer would be made.

Tracey rehearsed the names as she wove through the redcaps and passengers who were streaming across the big echoing, tile-floored lobby. Despite her sense of keyed-up and highly enjoyable importance at being here on such a mission, she also felt a dim foreboding.

"Tracey!" As she hastened through swinging doors onto the vaster, more open outer platforms, she heard her own name being shouted. "Tracey! Over here!"

Surprised, she saw Liz and the gang lined up before one of the gates. "Express for Baltimore, Wilmington,

Philadelphia, Trenton, Newark, New York, now ready on Track 5," the announcer's voice was droning. And it dawned on her — of course! This must be the day they were all leaving for the house party at the Cadells' place on the beach.

They all looked so cool and trim in their sun dresses, so alluringly gay and sophisticated with their tennis rackets and beach bags and luggage piled about their feet. Tracey trudged over with mixed emotions, and was lavishly embraced.

"To think you'd take time off from all the ailing dogs and cats and ocelots to wish us *bon voyage!* How is Harry, by the way? She's got this tame ocelot — imagine." Liz explained. "Carries him around like a kitten."

"All I'm interested in is how's this Whitney?" cried Joan Hampton. "How can you bear to tear yourself away? Liz says he's a real dream."

"To tell the truth I came to pick up a dog," Tracey told them, wishing acutely she had not entrusted Liz with the secret of her hopeless passion. But there was something bitterly lonely about not being able to confide in at least one girl.

"Wouldn't you know!" Mitzy Miller laughed. "Tracey, what've you done to your *hair?*"

"Like it?" One brown hand flew to it in sudden recollection. She had learned long ago that the safest thing to do was brag about your oddities, make them fun. "Real doggy, huh? I think I'll call it the Mange Dip Clip — start a fad."

They laughed joyously, and Liz clung to her arm. "No kidding, Trace! We sure wish you were coming along."

"Yeah, Trace," they told her. "You'd sure pep things up nights when the fellows aren't around."

An attendant opened the gates, and, laughing and

chattering and shoving, they began filing through, showing their tickets. "I'm not getting on," Tracey told the
trainman, waving her slip, and this information that had
once seemed rather impressive now was more a humiliating admission. "I'm just picking up a dog."

Waving cheerfully to her friends, who were clambering
onto a coach, Tracey hastened self-consciously toward
the forward section of Pullmans. It was a long walk to the
Palisades. She was hot and growing nervous, and now
more than ever aware of a pungent aroma that could
be coming only from her. As for her mottled hair — to
the girls it might be amusing, but she wondered how it
would look to a Mrs. Geraldine Vaughn.

Most suddenly and agonizingly of all, she itched. The
fleas had started up a real campaign.

Stoically resisting the impulse to scratch, Tracey
scanned the windows and the cars that stretched, it
seemed, for blocks. Where were they? Was it possible, in
her excitement, that she'd picked the wrong track, the
wrong train? But, no, there it said plainly, *Golden Arrow*
and *Palisades*. There was a warning hoot from the mon-
strous diesel far ahead, the stir of impending departure.
Tracey's throat was dry, her knees queerly weak. Then
down the platform they came.

Tugging a tall, skinny, and anxious lady at the business
end of a leash was a tall, skinny, and very anxious French
poodle. The woman was, however, very smart with all
that Florida tan, and her blond hair was expertly tipped
here and there with the same mange-mahogany as
Tracey's. The dog had the show cut Tracey disliked —
pompon, pantaloons, and all — and he wore a bejeweled
collar.

"Now baby," the woman was begging, looking urgently
about. Spying Tracey, she was obviously taken aback.

"How do you do," she said. "You can't be the person from the hospital! I expected someone much older!"

"Yes, I'm afraid I am. But don't worry," Tracey said, "I'm quite capable —"

"Do be good to him," the woman broke in. "He's very sensitive. Poor baby, he hates to leave his mummy! He's been grieving and trying to get away and run back to me this whole trip."

"All abo-o-o-oard!"

"Good-by, baby! Be a good boy." The train started to roll, The woman, still waving and calling plaintively, was yanked swiftly one direction, while Tracey was being yanked swiftly another.

"Wait, boy, wait — slow down!" He was heavy, for all his shaved-down look. He was strong as an ox. It was all she could do to hang on. She was practically galloping behind him as the car with Liz and the girls flashed past. She had an impression of their laughing faces pressed to the window, and knew, furiously, what a spectacle she must make.

Worse, the dog kept howling as if in pain, and darting wildly right and left. This meant weaving in and out among people, in constant danger of either losing him or tripping somebody in the path of the leash. "Pardon me! Oh, I'm so sorry — Excuse us, please!" She'd have to do what Dr. Baldwin suggested — simply haul off and carry him to a cab. If she could get close enough! Summoning all her strength, Tracey pulled him up short on the leash and grabbed him.

Wow! Was he heavy! She staggered — she was so tired and embarrassed and mad and hot. But if Dr. Jane Baldwin, who weighed a scant hundred and ten, could do it, so could she. Panting and disheveled, she had started toward the taxi entrance when the dog made a sudden lunge.

68

Before she knew quite what was happening, he had spurted from her grasp like a guided missile, straight into the path of an oncoming cab.

There was a mass gasp, a shout, and the screech of brakes, as a light-suited figure dropped his bags to make a flying tackle from the crowd. Shaking, fully expecting the worst, Tracey plowed forward.

"Whew, that was close!" Still kneeling, the young man was trying to soothe both the cab driver and the dog. "Here, boy, you aren't hurt — stop shaking, Now, now, now —"

He looked up into Tracey's white face. He was rangy and brown and extremely good-looking, with the lightest, clearest, gentlest blue eyes in the world, and a full-lipped, rather whimsical mouth.

"Hi! You the owner?" He stood up, all six feet four of him, and began to slap his knees and mop his brow. "This is some dog!"

"Thank you. I — I can't thank you enough."

"Where to, Miss? Where y'going?" the cabbie demanded.

She told him the Georgetown address, and the cabbie barked, "Georgetown. Anybody else for Georgetown?" and her rescuer said, "I am." He looked questioningly at Tracey. "If you don't mind?"

"Oh, no! It's customary to share the ride in Washington. In fact I'd feel better if you did."

For some silly reason she wanted to cry. She had to look hard out of the window, while gripping the leash tight, tight, in her scrubby brown fists. She hated it that her hair was spotty. She hated the tangy smell she gave off in the heat. This tall, easygoing stranger who sat hugging his knee in the crumpled seersucker suit kept looking at her kindly, yet so oddly. She felt terribly self-conscious, being looked over in such an open, yet sort of sympathetic, puzzled, and pondering way.

"I'm afraid your poodle —"

"It's not my poodle," she blurted. "I just work for a vet who's going to board him." Then, feeling as if she owed him some further expression of her gratefulness: "Thank you again. Dr. Baldwin's wonderful, but there's a limit. I — I'd never have the nerve to go back if I lost another dog."

"Another one?"

"Yes, I let a dachshund get loose my very first day, and he hasn't been heard from since."

"That is tough luck!"

"So you can see you not only saved this dog's life but in a way mine too!"

"I'm just glad I was there. You sure you can manage now?" They had pulled up before the hospital.

"Oh, sure! It's only a few steps. Come on, Pierrot." By coaxing and boosting and maneuvering, she managed to get the frightened, reluctant dog out of the taxi and steered in the proper direction. The blue-eyed stranger had sprung out himself and gallantly held open the hospital door.

"Good-by," Tracey said self-consciously. And hoping he wasn't getting too strong a whiff of her mixed aromas, she hastened past him, wishing suddenly and quite acutely that this wasn't good-by at all.

Dr. Baldwin looked up from the front desk where she was conferring with Mrs. Phillips. "Hullo, you look in the pink," she remarked, and came over to pat the still frantic, whimpering Pierrot. "I can't say as much for your dog. Have any trouble?"

"A — a little," Tracey acknowledged. "He seems to be pretty temperamental and scared of people." She swal-

70

lowed. " But it turned out O.K."

" Well, I've got good news for you, Tracey. Take Geraldine Vaughn here back and make him comfortable, then come into my office."

Puzzled but pleased, Tracey got her cringing charge safely settled in a kennel. For all the trouble he'd given her, her heart went out to him. " Don't worry, boy! We're all your friends — you'll like it here, I promise. Won't he, Butch? " She paused to give her former enemy a brisk head-scratching, and he practically wagged his tail off in delight.

Whitney, busy at the examining table, looked up as she spurted back past. His lips went down at the corners a shade. Even this perverse man's smile was upside down! But it added to her general sense of relief and success and better things to come.

" Hey! You heard? "

" No, what? " Tracey begged, her curiosity mounting.

" Whit, don't you dare! " the doctor called from her inner sanctum. And Whit shrugged and said, " O.K., go on, beat it."

The door stood open, and, even as she approached, Tracey could see the sight of all sights divine — Mrs. Frederick, holding a dashshund. And out of all the identical dachshunds waddling along on their short legs, this was, it could only be —

" Heidi! " Tracey cried, beside herself with joy and relief. " You found her! "

" Yes, she turned up on the doorstep last night. Where she's been we'll probably never know, but somebody must've been feeding her — look how fat she is. Rascal, you rascal, running off and worrying us so! " she scolded fondly, and the dog waggled all over and yapped and cocked its foolish head.

71

"Well, I certainly am glad." Tracey heaved the second biggest sigh of her life. The biggest had been just a few moments ago. "I can't tell you how awfully relieved I am!"

"We all are, Tracey," said the doctor, perching on the edge of her desk. "And I thought you might like to know things will be a little easier for you shortly. Diane — the girl I spoke of earlier, remember? — writes that she'll be able to come help us out after the first session of summer school. You won't have to be running your legs off quite so much as you have."

"Oh, that's fine. That's just — wonderful," Tracey managed, though, coming so unexpectedly, on the heels of everything else, it was, for some reason, a blow. She had a sudden sense of loss and stunned letdown.

Another girl! Ashamed of her own reaction, Tracey went back to work. Hectic though the pace, she'd enjoyed being the only one. The men liked her, as men so often did. Even their kidding, the practical jokes they played on her, had been in the spirit of comradeship. Another girl would spoil all that — she knew it instinctively. Especially someone who knew them better than she did, she remembered with a jealous pang, who'd worked here before.

As for Whit! Chill fingers gripped her heart. Any girl in her right mind would be mad for him. And one who was older, who'd had more experience — A girl with a name like Diane —

Chapter 7

DUDLEY CALLED for her in his car that evening, as usual. Welcome though the ride, Tracey was never exactly overjoyed to see him. She was uncomfortably conscious that his addiction to loud shirts — a Hawaiian number tonight with purple pineapples — added to his general appearance of juvenility, despite his scholarly mien.

Whit, now, had quiet taste. The few ecstatic glimpses she'd had of him off duty were in shirts of plain dark colors, say chocolate or gun metal, with a light sports coat. And Whit wouldn't have been caught dead in those Indian moccasins Dudley had made as an Eagle Scout. As for that ridiculous red corduroy hat with the feather that Dud was lazily twirling on his knees —

Torn, Tracey had to look away. She was stubbornly, passionately loyal, and she would have shed blood rather than hurt anybody's feelings, especially an old pal like Dudley. But it would be simply too excruciating if people here got the idea that Dud was her steady boy friend.

It eased her anguish, if but slightly, that Whit was listening with such patient respect to Dud's account of his leukemia experiments.

"And you say the pharmaceutical company sends you these mice, and you inject them with the cortisone and other preparations and report your findings? That's quite a deal. Tracey, why didn't you tell me your friend was a biochemist?"

"I don't know, I guess I haven't had the chance."

"Come out to the garage where I've set up my lab some

night, and I'll show you," Dud invited. And, seeing an opportunity, Tracey pounced on it.

"Yes, do, please. Last year I helped him," she explained. "We really put a lot of work into it, didn't we, Dud? And you both could stay for dinner — at our place, I mean."

"Better make it soon," advised Dud, clapping the silly hat on the back of his crisp yellow hair. "Your grandmother sent me down to warn you — she's already packing. You've got to get out of that apartment fast."

"But how come?" Tracey stood, astonished. "We got rid of all the pets!"

"Eloise showed up in the laundry tubs this afternoon."

"Eloise!" Her heart rejoiced an instant before it sank. "This seems to be my day for things coming back. Any — casualties?"

"Well, luckily no little old ladies. But Mr. Abbott happened to be washing out a pair of socks. I heard him yelling: 'Get the hoe! Bring me an ax!'"

"Oh, no!"

"Who's Eloise? A boa constrictor?" Whitney asked.

"No, just a beautiful, harmless black snake," Tracey told him. "Oh, I hope he didn't kill her!"

"I got there in time," said Dudley. "And while I hate to brag, Mark Antony's speech had nothing on mine."

"His was a funeral oration!"

"Mine was a prevent-the-funeral oration, and I'm happy to say it worked. Mr. Abbott's only stipulation was that you all get out."

"Must you be so blunt?" Tracey glanced anxiously at Whit. Dud could be very sweet and helpful, but tact was certainly not one of his charms. "The dinner invitation still stands. We'll find another place soon — we'll have to."

"No, thanks." Whit perched on the desk, laughing quite amiably but shaking his head. "Not if Eloise is

74

hanging around. A snake is one creature I don't care to have anything to do with."

Tracey turned to Dudley. "That's right — what about Eloise?"

"She's out in the car. I really couldn't take her to the lab, Trace. She might eat the white rats. And the zoo won't have her — I tried. I thought maybe the kindest thing would be to drop her off in Rock Creek Park."

"Yes. Yes, she'd probably be happier there than in another apartment. Or say — maybe we could get a house!"

They bought an *Evening Star* on the corner, and Tracey desperately read the "For Rent" ads while Dud cruised along shady, not too populous byways of the park, looking for a likely spot to turn Eloise out to pasture. They'd agreed it would be better this way — for Tracey not even to watch. She might weaken at the last minute, and Dudley had sternly advised against that.

"Your mother's been through enough already, Trace. I don't believe I'd add any more complications. After all, if you do find a house with a yard, you'll be able to take the dogs back."

Yes, Dud had a head on his shoulders, for all his silly shirts and hats. Dud had a lot of understanding. Tracey didn't even look up when he stopped the car and trudged quietly around to the back. Fervently she forced herself to concentrate on "Houses for Rent" in the ads.

"A house?" her mother cried, pacing the floor. "You must be out of your senses. I can't afford to rent a house, not if you expect to go to college!"

"Now, dear, now, Ellen," Grandmother soothed. Puffing, she dragged a suitcase from the closet and heaved it onto her quilted-satin bedspread. Reaching indiscriminately about, she began loading it with books, a clock, a corset. "That's not what we had in mind. We thought possibly we could rent a house with a nice big yard. Or say" — she turned on sudden inspiration to Tracey — "maybe a nice little acreage where we could keep a cow! I've always wanted to learn to milk, and think of the money we'd save."

"Mother, will you be sensible?" Her daughter-in-law whirled from the window, where she'd been clasping her brow, distraught. "And will you please stop that packing? We simply cannot be out of this apartment by the end of the week. In fact, we cannot be bullied out of it at all. It's not our fault that that — *thing* didn't go ahead and drown the way it should have! Tracey got rid of her pets. We are now living up to the terms of our lease."

"But the dogs!" Tracey pleaded. "We've got to find a place for the dogs. Mr. Cadell told me so, in no uncertain terms, when I went over to feed them tonight."

"Houses are not only scarce around Washington, they're sky high," Ellen Temple went on. "Besides, no sane person would rent us a house, with two dogs and a cat."

At that moment Aunt Azalea hallooed from the vestibule. "May I come in? May I come in? Dears, I've been thinking this whole situation over, and I have reached a decision." With playful deliberation she thrust her big ugly bag with its leering, lifelike alligator straight at Grandma, who was so startled she screamed and dropped a jar of cold cream. Tonight Aunt Azalea wore a big basket hat laden with the pink silk azaleas that were almost her trademark, pink net gloves, and a pink lace dress. She was really a dear, bright-eyed, remarkably pretty old lady, very feminine, as in her own lumbering way, her sister was. And, of course, Mother. And it trailed forlornly through Tracey's mind even now that it was

76

odd, come to think of it, that three such feminine women should have such a boyish relative.

"If it's coming to live with you and all those cats," Ellen said briskly but firmly, "thanks very much, Aunt Azalea, but — no thanks."

"I was afraid you'd take that attitude." Azalea commenced to inspect and rearrange the assortment of items Grandmother had dumped into the bag. "Sister, how you pack! I remember when we were girls and going to camp or abroad, I always had to come in and do your bags all over."

"Well, we're not girls and we're not going abroad or to camp. We are simply going — " Grandmother Temple paused. "My goodness! Where are we going?"

"To my place in Georgetown and no arguments," Aunt Azalea went on, efficiently rolling the corset around the clock, and stuffing stockings and underwear and lotions into the toes of shoes. "I have plenty of room in that big house, as you know, and the neighbors are quiet."

Tracey gave her mother a plaintive glance and grinned. "The neighbors should be — they're dead."

"Precisely," Aunt Azalea said. "It's so peaceful up there on the hill overlooking the cemetery. And the grounds make an excellent place to walk dogs."

"It cannot be peaceful any place where there are sixteen cats!"

"Only fifteen now, Ellen. We lost Archy. He came in all torn up one morning about two A.M. I called the hospital," Aunt Azalea told Tracey, "and the night man said to bring him right in. But before I could even back the car out, I could see it was — too late."

"I'm so sorry." Tracey patted her shoulder as Aunt Azalea resignedly dabbed at her eyes.

"Only fifteen," the aunt went on, "counting Ornrietta.

77

Who misses you awfully, by the way — just droops around. Ellen, I do think you should realize this child ought to be with her cat. And those dogs — how can you possibly deprive this poor child of them?"

"Please at least consider it, Mom," Tracey urged. "It'd be so close to the hospital for one thing. Why, think how much closer it'd be even to the FBI!"

"From my point of view it's a selfish offer, really," Aunt Azalea reasoned generously. "Tracey could help me with the cats. Just think of it — having trained veterinary help right on the premises."

"No," said Ellen emphatically. "Thank you kindly, but no. Tracey, give me that paper — let me see those ads!"

With mixed emotions, Tracey heard her mother furiously dialing real-estate companies. She managed to locate information on one house that could be seen yet tonight, and Aunt Azalea volunteered the use of her ancient but still cat-shiny, cat-smooth, purring Packard.

"Come on, Tracey, let's go at least see what they're offering to rent these days for a month's salary." Mrs. Temple tossed a white sweater across her shoulders, picked up her purse. "Mother, you two take any telephone messages carefully, if anybody calls. I've been wondering why we haven't heard from Jeff Carter."

That's right — Jeff! Tracey suddenly remembered. His father had written her mother way last month that Jeff might be coming out for a summer term at one of the universities, and that if so he'd be in touch with them. In her preoccupation with the new job, Tracey had almost forgotten. But now the awed excitement she had felt when her mother first mentioned the possibility struck afresh. What would it be like to see him after so long?

It was a little like her dream of finally meeting the great Dr. Baldwin — almost too incredible a marvel to expect.

Tracey and her mother decided to take the steps rather than wait for the elevator, and in a few minutes they drove off. Meanwhile, the two older women left off wrangling over the proper packing of a suitcase and decided to go call on some other old ladies in the apartment house.

The telephone began to ring the moment they stepped out.

To Tracey's delight, Whit took a remarkable turn for the better during the next few days. "Y'know," she was able to inform Dud, "I think he's beginning to like me."

"How come?"

"Well, he doesn't sneer any more when he looks at me!"

"Well, good."

"And this morning he actually paid me a compliment. He said: 'Well, well, what've you done to yourself? You don't look quite so horrible today.'"

Dudley took another look at her himself as he drove through traffic. "I've never thought you especially horrible-looking, Tracey."

"That's just because you've never especially looked at me, period. To you I'm just a — a signal on the other side of the wall or something. A noise, and sometimes a nuisance, but something you're used to — like your microscope. A — a kind of all-around, overgrown white rat."

"I wouldn't say white rat, exactly. Now that night I took you to the prom, you looked more like a — like a — "

"Yes, yes, go on!" Tracey urged, panting for a compliment, even from Dud.

"I don't know — It's hard to express it. You had on this

yellow dress, remember? With all the little holes in it. And you wore that brown fur wrap you had borrowed from your great-aunt."

"It was mink," Tracey informed him. "Real mink. And the dress was eyelet. And you're making me sound like a Swiss cheese on rye!"

"Well, since you put it like that, you looked real tasty," Dudley grinned. "But tasty wasn't the word I had in mind. It was more like — well, the feeling you get when an experiment works, when you find the bug you've been looking for wriggling around there on a slide!"

Tracey laughed. "Dud, that's sweet. That was a good try. I know exactly what you mean. And I guess if I can make an impression like that on a boy I've kicked around with as long as I have with you, I've at least got a chance with Whit. The only trouble is," she confided dolefully, "he's not likely ever to see me except in a sloppy apron, covered with dog hairs and fleas, at that!"

Whatever the reason, something had definitely come over Whit. His tough, strong, forbiddingly handsome face sort of — glowed. Tracey had actually surprised him humming under his breath. Even insults were tinged with benevolence. And the very next evening as she was leaving he found he was free to leave too, and suggested that they stop in the drugstore up the street and have a Coke.

She could hardly believe that she was floating along the sidewalk beside him, and then wriggling into a smooth, cool, apple-green upholstered booth. The drugstore was one of those with murals and glass brick and piped-in music, making you feel festive, as if it were a nightclub instead of a place where you could buy everything from Vaporub to garden hose. Making you feel downright romantic.

Whit, however, just sat there, not paying much atten-

80

tion to her but humming softly in his throat and sort of looking around. "What's this boy friend's name?" he came out with suddenly. "*Dudley?*" He made it sound awful, like another of his wry, mocking jokes.

Good — it flashed delightedly through Tracey — maybe he's jealous! But on the very heels of that she bridled. She felt very protective toward Dudley. "Well, it's no worse than Whitney, for heaven's sake!"

"Who said it was?" He grinned maddeningly. "Who said I had any burning fondness for my name?"

"That's right — Whitney's your last name, isn't it?" Tracey fumbled, feeling at a disadvantage. "What's your first?" she demanded.

"Wouldn't you like to know?"

"Oh, you're impossible." He was too much for her. All his maturity and sophistication, all his superior, caustic charm! Yet she had to, she must, bring him to heel. It had become a goading need. "Dud's a wonderful kid," she defended him. "Loyal, dependable, and not only phenomenally brilliant but he can be fun. But he's not," she said firmly, "my boy friend."

"You seem awfully anxious to reassure me of that."

"Do I?" She was forced to meet the prancing challenge 'of his eyes — "O.K., all right, so I am."

She had one ghastly moment when she was afraid he was going to ask her why. If he had, there was no help for it. She was too basically honest. She would have had to blurt out the humiliating truth: "Because I'm so desperately in love with you, that's why."

He didn't, however. He seemed to check the question at his very lips, and laughed instead. "What do you cut your hair with, a lawn mower?"

"No, a razor blade."

"I thought so. And comb it with an egg beater?"

81

"Don't make fun of me, Whit, please."

"I'm sorry. I get going sometimes and don't know when to quit. I torment people, I guess, because I'm a very tormented guy."

"You? Tormented?" She gazed at him incredulously. A man with his looks, his perverse charm. She had noticed how women clients fluttered over him. And it had been a source of both pain and pride the way rich young debs, especially, tried to get his attention, hung needlessly around him. She grimly enjoyed protecting him from their advances, being the one who could pick up their dogs and march through the door marked No ADMITTANCE by his side.

She said, because she hardly dared admit what she'd been thinking, "But, my goodness, with your prevet college work behind you and this terrific job — why, you're Dr. Baldwin's chief assistant, and at your age!"

"That's only the half of it. I've got a long way to go, Tracey, and I get pretty lonesome and discouraged."

Lonesome! Discouraged! Her heart pounced upon these unnecessary states. Let me help, it was pleading. Let me take care of that. But she musn't be like Dud, barging in, blurting out. That was often her trouble — being too direct and importunate, too eager. No, there were subtle ways of handling these things — modest, feminine ways that seemed to be fluttering all about her on elusive, shimmering wings. If only she could catch them, turn them brightly to her purpose! If only she could be deft, expert, maneuvering him into the design for him that would fit them both so beautifully!

But it was all too baffling. She'd never really had to work on a boy like this before. In fact, she'd never actually cared enough about anybody to put any effort into it.

"I'm sorry," he said before she could get any technique

or possibly effective remarks arranged. "I can't stand these lugubrious characters who spill their souls to anybody who'll stop, look, and listen."

Anybody! So she was just — anybody? Yet she mustn't be so sensitive, read disdain into everything he said.

She insisted: "Whit, you're nice. You're not a lugubrious guy, and you haven't tormented me. You've been awfully — nice to me. Why, the things I've learned from you!"

"You've caught on fast. You're a bright kid and you've simplified my job enormously. And to show my appreciation, I intend to buy you the biggest banana split in the place."

Kid! Banana split. "Thanks, but I'd rather have a cup of coffee," she said proudly. It was something just to be here, she kept telling herself. And if she didn't lose her head, louse things up — "I wouldn't want to spoil my dinner," she hinted broadly.

"That's right, your folks'll probably have it ready. I musn't keep you."

"Oh, Grandma wouldn't care!" she assured him. "I could call her. She's very understanding. And my mother's working tonight at the office. I could call her too if I wanted to stay down."

He looked taken aback, and now she'd done it. She'd overplayed her hand — wouldn't you know it!

He glanced at his watch. "I can't kill too much time myself. I'm doing some work at the Library of Congress. I usually go over and study till they close up, then eat late."

"Maybe you'd better have the banana split then," she said. And that's exactly what he ordered. And watching him dip the long spoon into its gooey mounds, she wished desperately she hadn't tried to be so sophisticated.

The nourishment seemed to restore his earlier spirits.

He was humming again as he steered her through the revolving door. He even took her arm, walking her to the bus stop along the street which was bathed in a pink sunset glow and alive with people hurrying home from their offices after a good day's work. Starlings sang their naughty songs in the trees and strung themselves along the white ledges of buildings like unwanted black jewels, and everything seemed errant and gay and promising.

"Thanks so much, Whit," she told him. "I've really enjoyed it."

"So have I. Glad old diligent, devoted Dudley didn't show up."

She winced, but she let it go. She didn't want to make too much of it, not if there was still the possibility that Whit might be encouraged by competition, even that of Dud.

And then, as the bus drew up, he came out with it, as if it were something that had been running just beneath the surface of everything all along. "I guess in another week or two things'll be different at the hospital — with Diane around."

"Diane?" Tracey was so surprised she couldn't think for a minute whom he meant. She looked up from pawing her purse for a bus token.

"The daughter of Dr. Baldwin's friend. I guess you'll be glad to have somebody else to help out."

"Well, I — hadn't thought too much about it. We seem to be getting along O.K. What's she like?" she asked.

A queer look came over his face, a look half of pain and half of wonder. He drew a deep, troubled breath. "She's beautiful," he said.

Chapter 8

THIS LAST REMARK, with its frightening implications, Tracey simply refused to think about. Like the problem of moving — they were still madly hunting a suitable spot — she put it resolutely out of her mind and gave herself over to making the most of her new relationship with Whit.

She could hardly wait to get to work. And she had never loved all the noisy, suffering, or merely fractious animals she attended to so much. Human love seemed to sharpen her senses, made her aware in wondrous new ways of much that she had accepted before. And love gave her courage.

She no longer felt weak or doubtful about Butch. Jake had been right — Butch was merely trying in his bellicose way to get her to love him. She had forced herself to pet him, and nearly wept the first time he nuzzled her hand. The next day, with Jake in close attendance, she had led him out into the big stone building across the court that held the exercise runs. And Butch had trotted along beside her, gentle as a fawn. On his release, she had laughed to watch his mad dash to the far end, wheeling so fast he almost stumbled, then tearing back, barking his lungs out, but all as if to impress her, to show off his marvelous strength and speed.

After that he nearly wagged his hind end loose at the sight of her, and whenever he was being brought back would make a beeline for her, planting his huge paws on her shoulders and almost knocking her down in his zeal to lick her face.

85

"Well, you're about the only one he likes around here," Whit complained, and that was the only flaw. When you love somebody you want everything else you love to love him. " Butch hates the sight of me and he always will."

"That's because you won't give him a chance. If you'd just — unbend, give things a — a — more of a chance to love you, Whit, not keep yourself locked away so tight."

It was presumptuous of her, she supposed, and she held her breath to see how he was taking it. But he only turned away with a shrug. He was so moody, she couldn't understand him, kidding and almost flirtatious one minute, depressed and curt the next. But nothing could dim the fact that she was making progress. Twice more he deigned to treat her at the drugstore, and almost every noon he'd saunter into the lounge where she was munching her sandwiches and pour her a cup of the bitter black coffee that he always let perk too long. But it was also bracing and darkly exciting, like Whit himself, and she drank it as ambrosia and praised it to the skies.

He would hurl himself on his spine beside her on the leather couch, and sipping his own coffee — he never seemed to eat — smile to watch her playing with Hi Fi, a dear little Peke they were boarding, to whom she'd taken a desperate fancy. Hi Fi would stand up and beg so charmingly for bites of sandwich, would dart so frantically after the ball she tossed. Whit lost his sardonic, troubled look, watching her play with the dog and teach it tricks. His laugh rang out.

She was learning, gradually, more about him. Evidently his folks were separated. He didn't say much about them, only that his father was angry that Whit had decided on veterinary medicine instead of the other kind, and had withdrawn all financial help in the hope that he'd still change his mind. " He just can't see me as a horse doctor,

86

as he calls it, stuck out in the sticks."

"But you wouldn't have to be," Tracey said, this day he'd volunteered so much. She caught Hi Fi onto her lap and cuddled the perky, panting bundle of furry flesh. "Why, you could have your own city hospital someday, like this."

"City hospital? Are you kidding? Treating dogs and cats is the last thing I want. What I really want is a farm, with lots of horses and cows and pigs — the works. With somebody else to run the place maybe while I go out and work on other people's stock."

Tracey was so delighted that she sat bolt upright, letting Hi Fi slide to the floor. This fitted into her plans just great! "Why, that's exactly what I've always dreamed of myself!" she exclaimed. "Only mine would be more of a ranch. Raising blooded horses —"

He wasn't listening, however. Now that he'd started, he was interested only in talking about himself. "My mother couldn't care less," he went on. "She's a great beauty — it's her claim to fame. She lives out in Carmel, California, and entertains the movie stars, which is the next best thing to being a movie star herself. Being beautiful and having the money to hobnob with the great — that's her dish. Boy! Have you ever noticed how cold beautiful women are?"

"Well, no. No, I've always thought — well, like everybody else, I guess I've always envied them."

"Don't. They're never happy, Tracey. As for the men in their lives — All I can say is it's a disaster being mixed up with a beautiful woman, whether she's your mother or anybody else."

"Thank goodness I'm not beautiful then."

Tracey bleakly realized he was just sounding off. But she didn't know whether to be flattered by his confidence

87

or rebuffed. It — maybe it only went to show how inconsequential she was to him.

When a man doesn't even challenge your statement that you know you're not beautiful, when he doesn't even seize the opportunity to tell you at least you have your points, when he just lets you go on sitting there, playing with a dog! Oh, it was all too complicated, being in love with such a person! It was almost better before, when the only attention he paid her was to bawl her out.

The buzzer rang that evening as Tracey was clearing the dishes. It had been a hectic meal. Aunt Azalea had descended in full feather during dessert, and Mother, worn down by the hopeless hunt of the past week had finally yielded to her offer of at least temporary shelter. What actually tipped the scales was the fact that Littlebit and Cricket were back. Mr. Cadell, who was locking up the house to join the family at the shore, had delivered them bodily that afternoon.

The dogs, wild with delight at what seemed to them their home-coming had been tearing all over the apartment, yapping and cavorting and leaping onto beds and rooting out old toys. Short of actually knocking them on the head, there seemed no way to keep them quiet. It was only a matter of time, everybody nervously realized, before the manager would appear.

"That can't be Mr. Abbott," said Mrs. Temple as the buzzer sounded again. "He'll just come banging on the door."

"Probably some salesman," said Grandmother. "I declare there's no escaping them — they even pester you on the phone. I've gotten so if I don't know the voice right off I just say, 'I'm sorry, young man, I don't need any magazines, and I'm too old to accept your bargain offer for dancing lessons,' and just hang up."

"Mother, you don't!" protested Ellen. "Why, it might be somebody important."

"That's right — say somebody from the hospital," said Tracey, at least beating her to the speaking tube. "Hello?"

"Is this the Temple apartment? This is Jeff Carter. I've been trying to get in touch with somebody out here for days."

"Jeff! It's Jeff — Jeff Carter!" she screamed, pressing the lock release. "Come on up!"

Unable to wait, she ran into the hall, the dogs bounding recklessly after. And in a minute a tall figure in a seersucker suit stepped off the elevator. Tracey stared at him, astounded. "Why, you — but you — This is too fantastic."

He clapped a hand to his brow, equally stunned. "The taxi! The girl with the dog in the taxi. Why, you met my train!"

Laughing, shaken by this incredible discovery, they burst back in on the others to explain. "Jeff's been in town for two weeks. He saved my life, at least my dog's life, the very first day he came. We even rode in the same cab and never had the faintest idea —"

"I thought she looked familiar — something about her. I kept trying to figure out who she reminded me of."

"You kept staring at me, that's for sure." Tracey remembered now, with horror, her smell and speckled hair. "Of course, I can hardly blame you — I'd just had a run-in with a mangy collie."

Jeff laughed joyously. His teeth flashed white in his long bronzed face, and his blue eyes sparkled. There was something big and shining and uncomplicated about him — rugged as mountains, clear as a cold brook, clean-swept as a plain.

Tracey's mother had to stand on tiptoe to hug him,

that's how tall he was. "Jeff, Jeff! We've been expecting to hear from you. Why didn't you get in touch with us?"

"Believe me, I've tried. But you seem to have an answering service that says, 'Wrong number,' or 'No, thanks, young man, I do not want to learn to rumba!' or doesn't answer at all. I finally decided the only thing to do was to barge out here and see if you were still in town."

Unflustered, Grandmother apologized. "I'm sorry. But then you can't be too careful," she reasoned. "Not with a pretty girl like Tracey in the house."

"Oh, Grandma!" Tracey wailed.

"She's right, dear," Aunt Azalea chimed in. And in a flash of awful perception, Tracey saw that they were going to try to impress Jeff with her charms. "Why, so many boys are continually calling Tracey that they're moving in with me to escape."

"She means we're moving because we're being kicked out," Tracey corrected bluntly. "On account of the pets. We're expecting the management up any minute."

"Boy!" Jeff grinned. "A good thing I caught you when I did."

"It certainly is," said Grandma Temple. "We're very glad you did. In fact I like you — I even liked your voice over the phone. It was all I could do to restrain myself from saying, 'Young man, if you're going to teach them I'll take those dancing lessons'."

"But he wasn't selling any dancing lessons, Grandma!"

It was all too hopeless, but it didn't seem to matter. Looking bewildered but amused, Jeff draped his immense frame in a chair, caught Cricket when she bounded to his lap, and half yielding to her caresses, half deflecting them, managed to get his long pipe lighted.

With the matter of a destination settled, the two older

90.

women plunged into joyful new gestures of packing, while Tracey and her mother and Jeff tried to catch up on ten years of news.

"Rick married right out of high school and he and Bill are helping Dad run what's left of the ranch — we sold off half of it a few years ago. Clem's a freshman and I'll be a junior this fall at Wyoming. But as a political-science major I decided to take some special courses this summer at Georgetown."

"Political science?" said Ellen. "Why, Jeff, with your way with horses I always thought you'd be the one to run the ranch."

"Or a mining engineer," said Tracey. "Remember how we used to pan for gold?"

"I finally decided I'd never find it." He winked at her and nibbled his pipe. "Maybe I lost interest after I lost my po'dner. And a ranch can be a mighty lonesome place. I figure maybe I should stake out my claim a little farther, learn what I can about helping to run this crazy, mixed-up world."

"That's wonderful, Jeff," Ellen Temple said. "Heaven knows it could use some help. Maybe if more young men like you would dedicate their lives to world affairs, fewer of them would have to give their lives in world wars."

That's right, thought Tracey, fervently admiring both her mother and this attractive, clean-cut stranger. But she was also dismayed. She felt an acute pang of protest and disappointment, as before some unaccountable loss. As if some basic premise of her own existence had been swept away. Until right now she hadn't realized how strongly she had counted on one day returning to the ranch. The whole ranch, just as it had been, with Jeff there in his former role.

An older, taller Jeff, of course, but a Jeff as constant, as

91

unchanged as the mountains. Her first delight at discovering that he had been the stranger in the taxi had vanished. This wasn't Jeff at all — he was lost to her forever. Despite the reminiscences he was exchanging with Mother, this was an engaging, long-limbed stranger, whose coming had robbed her of something priceless and irreplaceable.

Toward eleven o'clock Aunt Azalea broke in, saying that if he lived in or near Georgetown, she'd take him home. "There's method in my madness," she twinkled. And before anyone could stop her, she had handed him a suitcase. "Since they're moving shortly and you have all those lovely muscles, you can carry a few things down."

"Oh, Auntie, no!" gasped Ellen, while the horrified Tracey tried to grab it from him.

"Nonsense." Grinning around his clenched pipe, he thrust her off, much as he had the dogs, and with the other hand accepted a bridge lamp, which Grandma, not to be outdone, had efficiently unplugged. "Makes me feel like one of the family. If I felt I wasn't after all those years of thinking about you and Tracey, Mrs. Temple — well, it'd be an awful letdown."

Tracey caught up the dogs, who didn't want to see him go. They had set up a frantic barking, and although it couldn't matter now, still, she didn't want the added complication of the landlord's appearing. Things were embarrassing enough. "Hush now, you two! Behave!"

"Bring them down to the car too, dear," urged Azalea. "It will simplify everything to get them out of here as soon as possible."

"Yes, please, for heaven's sake," pleaded Tracey's mother. And so, in a flurry of dogs, suitcases, and boxes, Tracey and the long-lost Jeff — or the intriguing, new-found stranger — crowded onto the elevator.

"Hey, hold it! Wait! What's up?" Dudley, always

nearsighted without his glasses, burst into the hall. "You eloping or something? Tracey, who is this joker?"

"Dudley, really!" Tracey scolded, outraged. "This is Jeff Carter. You know, from Wyoming. My — my almost brother."

"O.K., sorry. Put 'er there, Jeff. No offense intended."

"I'm sorry too, because I can't," grinned Jeff, indicating his full hands "But I don't blame you."

"Yeah, you see in a city this size with a girl like Tracey — can't be too careful."

"He's already had that line," Tracey said tightly. "Now will all my flaming avengers please get down off their horses and either get out of my way or give us a hand?"

That was a mistake, though, because Dud took her at her word and began to grab such items as an ironing board, which he carried cleverly turtle-fashion on his back, and a lampshade, which he cocked jauntily on his head, and they were stuck with him.

"Well, well, so you're finally moving, Trace?" Dud kept exclaiming forlornly. "I can't believe it. This kid's been like a sister to me too for going on ten years now," he explained.

"Well, everybody's luck has to run out sometime," Jeff said.

"Everybody's sister, nobody's sweetheart," Tracey cracked dryly, and her heart fled in a kind of protective desperation to Whit. Would she ever be anything but a kind of kid sister to him, either?

"Listen, don't let her fool you! She's got plenty-a guys on her trail," Dud claimed in mistaken loyalty as the boys set down their burdens on the sidewalk and tried to figure out which of Aunt Azalea's keys unlocked the trunk of the queenly old car. "Trouble is, she'd rather fool around with dogs and cats."

"How about horses?" Jeff got the trunk open and began to put things in. "Tracey did everything but eat and sleep with the horses back on the ranch."

"You have to be rich to ride out here," said Tracey. "The nearest I ever get to a horse any more is when a mounted policeman goes by in the park."

"Maybe we can do something about that," said Jeff.

Any boy with a lick of perception would have beat it, Tracey was thinking, but no, not Dud. He had to go on being helpful, hoisting the dogs into the car, and rolling up the windows, and asking: "Hey, where you moving to, anyway? Don't tell me you're really going to live with your aunt and all those cats?"

"Isn't that fairly obvious?" Tracey said coldly. "And if you were a gentleman you'd go back and see what else you can carry down."

"Oh, yeah, sure! I get it." Dud gave a knowing look at Jeff, shrugged, and, whistling, went obediently off.

"Honestly!" Tracey clutched her hair. "Jeff, I could just die. I guess it's a good thing you didn't know what you were getting into or you wouldn't have gone to all the effort to find us."

"Don't be silly. What're you talking about?"

"Oh — everything. The way everybody's acted, and having to move, and — and roping you in like this."

"Listen, you don't know what a relief it is. All this makes me feel at home. And the luckiest break of all is that you'll be only a few blocks from where I'm rooming — at least that's the way it looks from your aunt's address."

"Oh, yes, isn't that wonderful?" She was suddenly self-conscious. The words came out stiff and polite, not the way she wanted them to at all. "We do want to see a lot of you this summer, all of us. We — be sure to let us know if there's anything we can do for you while you're in town."

"Sunday dinners? Guided tours?" His brows went up a notch.

Chapter 9

To TRACEY'S ASTONISHED DISTRESS, when they officially moved a few days later, Jeff, of all people, was along. He clambered out of Aunt Azalea's car and helped Dudley and the movers lug down their furnishings. He still seemed a puzzling stranger, even in the sweat shirt and faded blue jeans. And this was so — intimate a task, somehow. Also, she was a little bit ashamed of the things Mother had decided to store in Azalea's garage. She hadn't realized before how battered their luggage was, how worn the chairs, or what havoc the dogs had played with the old green studio couch.

It was considerable compensation that Aunt Azalea's place was so impressive, however bizarre. Two weathered Egyptian stone cats guarded the iron gates before the Spanish stucco house overlooking the peaceful sweep of the cemetery. There were Orientals on the scratched parquet floors, and the draperies that hung at the tall windows with their iron grillwork were real, if faded, Chinese brocade. The whole place was cluttered and crammed with statues with broken noses, cracked Ming vases, Italian-marble fireplaces that didn't work, dusty, fat-bellied gods, teakwood tables, and ominous-sounding gongs. Unfortunately, pervading all this like a musky incense, was a strong aroma of cat.

Still, Tracey drew what reflected glory from it she

could. Her principal anxiety now was the strong suspicion that her aunt had roped Jeff into helping, the same as she had the other night.

"Really, Jeff, you musn't feel obligated to us," she told him, hastening to the door with him when the job was finally finished. "We know you'll be busy studying, and also you'll probably want to be with friends you've made, friends your own age. Just because it's turned out we'll be practically neighbors is no sign you've got to be monopolized."

Again, as before, he seemed taken aback. "Get this straight: I wanted to help. In fact, I want to see as much of you and your mother as I can. But I surely don't want to impose!"

"Oh, no, no!" She wailed. "Don't get that idea — it isn't that."

"It works both ways. I realize you're probably busy too, going out with, as you say, friends your own age."

"Most of my friends are out of town. And frankly," she told him bluntly, "kids my age and I don't have too much in common."

"I don't wonder, Tracey. Selfishly, I'm glad." He pressed her hand. "Well, good night."

Intrigued but faintly upset, Tracey turned back into the house. Was this really Jeff she'd been talking to? He still would not quite merge with the person of her memories. Yet there was something awfully promising about having a friend like that, a real man almost as old as Whit on the scene.

Whit! She still got all limp and distraught and thrilled every time she even thought of him. Either she'd have to make some progress with him soon or force herself to get over him. And the best way to do that, she guessed, was to become interested in somebody else. Well, one thing

96

sure, she had always been interested in Jeff Carter and always would be. His appearing right now seemed suddenly a godsend.

The very next morning, however, Whit did a very nice thing. He asked Dr. Baldwin if Tracey could be allowed to watch a Caesarean section. Tracey had long since confided her longing either to assist or observe in surgery, and Whit had told her emphatically to forget it. Now, all unannounced, as Tracey herself carried the cocker spaniel into the operating room, she heard him proposing, "How would it be if Tracey stuck around?"

Tracey was so surprised she almost dropped the patient. And to her further surprise, Dr. Baldwin looked up from the basin where she was scrubbing and said crisply: "What d'you think, Tracey? Can you spare the time?"

"Oh, yes, yes, I'm sure — if Whit thinks so."

"And how about you? Can you manage yourself, I mean?"

"You mean would I get sick? Oh, gracious no, not after all the wounds I've dressed!"

"All right, if you're positive. We have to use ether, you know — nembutal goes through the system and might affect the puppies. Don't stand too close, and if you should feel faint, go sit down on the floor near the window and put your head between your knees."

They had the dog on the table. Tracey helped to tie her down, while Whit prepared the ether cone. Standing carefully back, yet on tiptoe the better to watch the doctor's every skilled movement, Tracey waited. Her palms tingled. Suspense, delight, and wonder — plus a warm, glowing current of gratitude for Whit — coursed through her.

"Give her a little more. O.K., that's got it." The scalpel caught the light; the incision was small and neat; the

97

blood flowed onto the white padding, the cotton sponges. And Whit kept handing the doctor things. In a minute she lifted out a small, fat shining roll of living matter, which Whit placed in a box with a hot water bottle.

"There seem to be four," said the doctor, and looked up and smiled at Tracey. "How you doing?"

"Oh, fine, fine! It's so — so — beautiful!" Her voice sounded high and funny; their faces were looming and receding; the room began to rock. It wasn't the blood or anything like that — it was the ether. She had gotten closer than she realized, gotten quite a strong whiff of it. And suddenly, appallingly, Tracey was plunging through the door.

The next thing she knew somebody big and strong was catching her. And after that she was coasting back to consciousness on the couch in the adjoining room.

"You nut!" Whit scolded. "You idiot! Why didn't you sit down the way the doctor said?"

"There wasn't time. I had to get out of there!"

"Well, you didn't have to dive for the stairs, did you? In another minute you'd have broken your neck."

Tracey buried her face against his shoulder. She knew, for one blissful moment, his arms around her. He'd saved her life! But he'd also lost all respect for her — he'd never dare to go to bat for her again. As for Dr. Baldwin —

"It was stupid of me," Tracey said, head low. "I don't know when I've been so ashamed."

Dr. Baldwin was drying her hands thoughtfully, rolling down her white sleeves. "Yes, it was pretty stupid of you not to follow my orders. But then maybe it was stupid of me to let you come up in the first place."

"That's what I was afraid you'd think!" Tracey cried.

"We all do stupid things at times, Tracey. If it'll make

98

you feel any better, I flopped too once when I was a lot older than you. It was in vet school and we were dissecting a horse. It was a hot day, very close, and I wasn't feeling too well, and I was the only girl in the class. And if you think the fellows in vet school don't relish any signs of weakness in a girl, or the teachers themselves don't make it as rough on you as they can — do everything in their power, some of them anyway, to flunk you out — "

"I realize that," Tracey said.

"Well, just so you know what you're up against, the self-control it's going to take if you decide to go on."

"If I decide?" Tracey protested. "But there's not the slightest question — there never has been."

"There's a long time to change your mind yet. You might fall in love and get married."

Tracey flushed. "That'd work out O.K., I should think — if he happened to be in the same business."

The doctor flashed her a quick glance that made Tracey regret her words. The last thing she wanted was for Dr. Baldwin to detect her mad passion for Whit. "The right ones never are," the doctor laughed. "Well, come on, let's see how Mrs. McDougal's doing."

The dog on whom the Caesarean section had been performed that morning was not in actual pain, now that the anesthetic had worn off, but she was restless and uncomfortable, to say the least.

"Poor girl, this is her first litter, and I'm afraid she's not going to like it," said the doctor, "but those pups have got to nurse. Better bring them down, Tracey."

Anxious to be restored to grace, Tracey scurried upstairs and hastened down with the box. "There, there, boys! We know you're hungry, and dinner's coming right up," she crooned to its small blind, frantically whimpering occupants.

"Don't be too sure," Whit predicted, passing her on the steps. "That bitch is a nipper: she got me when she first came in." For the first time Tracey noticed his bandaged finger. "And I doubt if becoming a mother has improved her disposition any."

"I'm not worried," Tracey told him. Hugging the box to her bosom, she dared to catch his eye in an impish, shy little glory-filled glance. He had held her. He couldn't deny the fact that, however accidental, yes, even humiliating the circumstances, those marvelous arms had been around her.

And reading her meaning, he snorted, but his lips quirked. "Oh, for Pete's sake!" Half disdainfully, with a kind of exaggerated ardor, he held out his arms. "Anybody else care to fake a faint?"

Tracey was startled. He knew better, of course, but it was a low blow. She didn't know whether to laugh or trip him. For a second she was terribly tempted to send him crashing down the steps to land on his beautiful curly head.

"Coward!" she got in the verbal lick instead. "You're just scared of dogs. Especially females. Or is it females, period?"

He was scared of dogs too — Butch, anyway — there was some satisfaction in thinking. And Whit certainly wasn't much good with new or expectant mothers. Of course this was more — well, a woman's job, anyway — the whole business of loving and protecting and looking after some poor, panting creature who was having babies. A vast tenderness filled Tracey. If only she hadn't loused things up upstairs! But at least she was successful at introducing puppies to their mother, even ornery, reluctant mothers like this cocker.

"You sure you can handle her?" Dr. Baldwin asked.

"Oh, yes, we'll get along fine! Here's your family. Aren't they sweet?" Tracey said, addressing the dog. The dog snarled and would have attacked the proffered offspring. "I guess I'll have to get into the cage."

"Yes, she might try to eat them," said the doctor. "You'd better stick around."

Tracey unlatched the kennel and, talking softly to its growling mistress, crawled in. Her heart was pounding in a kind of high wonder, but she wasn't afraid. This was a challenge. She knew that most mothers of all species accept their young with such instinctive passion that they will kill to protect them. Yet nature has strange quirks: there are also others that must be kept from destroying their offspring. These must be taught acceptance; they must be taught the ways of love.

"It's all right, girl! It's all right." She soothed and fondled the still-fretful mother, and when she was quiet pressed one of the fat, hot, silken puppies to the nipple. How ravenous it was; how it tugged! "There now, there now —" Tracey took up its sister. It rooted about and in its blind frenzy lost hold. Patiently she helped it regain its grip. Soon all four were nursing lustily. And the mother, though lying listless and dour with her head on her paws, as if skeptical of the whole business, had at least been subdued.

Whit came up short in passing, stood regarding them with folded arms. "Well, picture of a happy little family. Sheer togetherness!"

Tracey smiled blissfully out at him. It was a pretty silly pose, she knew, perched on a cage floor like this with a lap full of guzzling pups. But his sardonic tone could not conceal the expression in his eyes. An expression she'd glimpsed before, when he'd gently taken these selfsame puppies from Dr. Baldwin's hands. Whit yearned for what psychologists would probably call a mother figure in his life. Well, she was so crazy about him she'd settle even for that. Though being like a mother to him wasn't exactly what she'd had in mind.

"See? I told you there's nothing to it." Tracey lifted one squirming, lop-eared bundle and held it to her cheek. "Nothing to be afraid of at all. Why, even Mrs. McDougal is getting to like the idea of having a family."

As if to prove it, the dog lifted her head, regarded Tracey for an instant, then turned and began to lick and nuzzle her babies for the first time.

At that very moment, however, the excitement began out front. "Somebody come out, please!" came over the loudspeaker. The voice was not Mrs. Phillips'. The voice was strangely like music, exultant and high and young.

Whit wheeled as if he had been struck. "Diane!" His face had paled. The word burst from him in a hoarse little cry. Then joyously shouting the name again, he charged toward the door.

From all over the hospital there seemed to be doors banging, people taking up the cry. Dr. Baldwin burst from her office, smiling. Jake hurried in from the exercise pens. Bert, in his big rubber apron, and with a wet pooch in his arms, left the bath tables to holler over the rail, "Tell her I'll be down as soon as I can." Even the dogs began to bark.

Tracey swallowed, stirred one cramped leg that had gone to sleep. Her mission had been accomplished. The puppies were making ecstatic little grunts as they nursed, the mother sinking into a reconciled sleep. She supposed she should rush out too, join the grand parade. But dread and dismay seemed to root her to the spot. And fear and an acute sense of protest.

102

It was as if, just as she'd reached so hopefully out at least to touch it, somebody else had dipped blithely in to snatch away the prize.

Chapter 10

DIANE OSBORNE was the kind of girl who inspired other girls simply to go jump quietly into the Potomac. She was so beautiful it hurt. For one thing, she was so petite. She was like a golden locket, whose very smallness makes it exquisite and so unutterably precious that you're almost afraid to wear it.

Her hair was a soft, silver-gold puff. Her skin was honey-colored. And her face, in all its distinctive, perfectly arranged proportions, was the kind of face people turn to gaze at just an instant longer on the street. It was as if, by being so beautiful, she was conveying a favor on others; as if her primary purpose in life was only to exist.

As if this weren't enough, she emanated a kind of golden radiance. Plainer people lighted up in her presence, as if basking in a glow. She wasn't particularly witty, but whatever she said, in a soft little voice of surprised amusement, made you want to smile. You felt yourself dissolving before her, wanting to please her, and that life would somehow be intolerable if you failed.

Then when you were rearing back in sheer self-defense, when you realized you'd have to hate her a little bit too, if only to survive, you noticed something else: when she turned, with a swish of her embroidered peasant skirt, and started across the office, you noticed the slight but definite limp.

For one black, unworthy instant, Tracey rejoiced. But hot on the heels of this bitter gloating, Tracey was ashamed. She could hardly stand herself. And also, she realized with a hopeless pang, Diane's handicap only added something poignant to her loveliness. How could you hate or even resent a girl who'd nearly died once of polio? It was the final, devastating fact that made you forgive her, that robbed you of any possible advantage.

Tracey escaped when the excitement of introductions had subsided, and plunged back into the kennel room. It was time for the dogs to be exercised, and she made instinctively for Butch. It was consoling the way he hurled his big strength against her, in an excess of sheer devotion. And while he was out, she set to cleaning cages with a vengeance.

After her first couple of weeks of being broken in, the men had done this for her. It was sort of understood. Today nobody came to her aid: they were simply too occupied with the returning wonder of Diane. O.K. — who cared? Tracey plunged a heavy-bristled brush into a pail of foaming disinfectant, attacked the kennel floor. But it was no use: there was simply no way to scrub away her own black jealousy.

Especially when the door swung open, and Whit seemed to levitate through. One look at him was enough to confirm her worst suspicions. His face managed to be both radiant and anguished, both alive in some tingling new way and slightly dazed. It was the look of a man in love, if she'd ever seen one, which, come right down to it, she guessed she never had.

"Well, hi, Tracey!" he exclaimed, as if they hadn't been in close contact all day. "Nice job."

Tracey sat back on her heels, thunderstruck. So that was it! It struck her now with staggering impact. The meaning of this recent change in Whit. His blunt, " She's beautiful," that night at the bus. And after that his moodiness. His lashing out so futilely at beautful women. And she had actually taken comfort, thought it helped her own cause. Oh, how stupid, absolutely deaf, dumb, and deluded could you get?

But even worse, more ghastly now in retrospect, was his cheerfulness. The times when he'd been gay and kind and funny, filled with a barbed, bright excitement. All that had been nothing but nervous anticipation. Or as if maybe, by being a very good boy, nice to old ladies and dumb animals and dumb girls, he might be worthy of a miracle like Diane!

Most disturbing of all to Tracey was the fact that, no matter how she steeled herself, she too melted in that golden presence. When Diane flipped back that nimbus of hair and emitted that flutelike laugh, you felt a reluctant surge of glory, you wanted to laugh back. When she asked you to do her a favor, like running upstairs with a message for Bert, or getting her fresh linen, or preparing the needles, you felt almost honored to accommodate. She was irresistible, that was all. Little and lovely and skillful, not only in everything she did, but in the many things she preferred to let you do for her. And besides — she limped. Whenever doubts and resentments and dark protests began to intrude, that undeniable fact accosted you, and you hated yourself.

To add insult to injury, Tracey could not console herself that Diane might be beautiful but dumb. The next day, while Tracey did mundane things like checking bath lists and taking temperatures, Diane and Whit worked together at one table. And it was Whit who humbly did the holding, while Diane, humming, gave the shots.

105

Tracey could not help pausing to observe. And as those deft, delicate fingers expertly plunged the needle, it was like a stab into her own breast. Tracey hadn't even been allowed to give shots, as yet. Of course, Diane was a second-year prevet student, but remembering that didn't help much.

One thing sure, something new had definitely been added to the hospital atmosphere: a subtle air of anticipation, as if any moment now the curtain would go up on scenes of romantic drama. The men whistled at their work. Mrs. Phillips beamed. Even Dr. Baldwin wore a tentative little half-smile, and, although her manner was vaguely reluctant, somewhat on guard, you sensed that even she was intrigued by the reunion of these two.

For reunion, of course, it was. Bert could hardly wait to get Tracey across from him at the bath tables before confiding: " It was some show last summer, I tell you! Crazy about each other one week, then, bingo! she'd drop him, and if ever you seen a whipped cur — "

" Whit could never behave like a whipped cur," Tracey defended hotly. " Don't you say such things about him. Besides, don't you know gossip is the lowest form of human endeavor? " She began furiously to towel-dry a quaking poodle. " What else do you know? "

" They was practically engaged once. She was wearing his class ring and his fraternity pin even. They could hardly get two inches apart — ate every meal together. Talk about a coupla sick calves — I tell you! " Bert chuckled with mock disgust, but his whole big rough, ruddy countenance relished the memory. Gently he began to comb the chow he had lifted from the dryer. " Then, bingo! it was all off again. Just like that she dropped him."

" But why? " protested Tracey. Her heart was breaking. Why had she let Bert torture her like this in the first

106

place? The picture he had painted of them together — the hopeless, beautiful picture. And she had imagined, she had had the stupid nerve to imagine people around the hospital were beginning to fancy a romance between herself and Whit! "Did Diane fall for somebody else?"

"Nope, nobody knows. But then there's no explaining women — crazy, unpredictable creatures the lot of 'em, Lord love 'em! But what'd we do without 'em?" He chuckled. "Of course," he added, wielding the comb, "Whit's an awful strong-minded, high-handed, possessive, gloomy kind of guy."

"He's nothing of the kind," Tracey retorted, half under her breath. She thrust her own dog into a dryer and set the switch. Detesting herself, she asked, "Do — what do you think about them this summer?"

Bert considered. Taking the long steel comb, he scratched his own bald head. "Whether or not she'll take up with him again is anybody's guess. But one thing sure, he seems to be asking for it, poor guy!"

It was true, all that Bert had said. The attitudes of everybody in the place confirmed it. And avidly, punishing herself, Tracey watched them together, and could have wept.

For Whit, the dour, the forbidding, the arrogant, had become Diane's abject slave. It was too disgusting, too — outrageous, to see him so reduced. Look at him, just look at him! Tracey fumed as he galloped around doing Diane's bidding, much as she, Tracey, had once dashed obediently about doing his; as he hung around her, sometimes rapturous, sometimes doleful, but always practically quivering, like a hungry dog awaiting any carelessly tossed scrap.

Tracey could hardly stand it. When you admire someone for his strength, even though that very factor may frighten and discourage you, it is like an assault on your

107

own spirit to see that strength dissolving, trickling absurdly away.

To Tracey's dismay and confusion, Whit treated her now like a kind of fond counselor and go-between. When things were going well, when Diane laughed and flirted with him and you saw them in serious conversation in corners, on days when instead of brewing black coffee for Tracey he was taking Diane to lunch, he would slip up behind Tracey and ask in his offhand manner — half-smiling, distant, as if allowing her a glimpse of something precious — "Isn't she absolutely the most beautiful thing you ever saw?"

Tracey looked up, this day, from perhaps the ugliest bulldog that had ever suffered a broken leg and asked deliberately, "Who — Duchess?"

He laughed softly. "You brat! You know exactly whom I mean."

"I thought you couldn't bear beautiful women. I thought you considered them your direst enemies!"

"Listen, Tracey — " He colored. She could see his fists go tight in the pockets of his white jacket, and for a minute she wished she could hand him Diane on a silver platter, if only to wipe that look of misery off his face. "We say a lot of things when we're hurt and can't have what we really want."

"I'm sorry. I shouldn't have thrown it up to you. I guess I'm just jealous."

She could have bitten her tongue off, she was so stricken by this admission. And he looked so startled and incredulous, if flattered too and vaguely amused.

"Of — of Diane's experience, I mean!" Tracey tried desperately to undo the damage. "Of how good she is, and her being allowed up in surgery and — and not fainting!"

108

Whit grinned wryly. "No, worse luck."

And at that moment Diane skimmed up behind them. Her limp gave her this queer, birdlike way of half walking, half skipping, that made her seem even more ethereal. In addition, she could imitate bird calls, and she gave a winsome little series of trills and chirpings now.

"What is this deep, dire huddle? And did I hear my name being taken in vain?"

Tracey braced herself, but there it was again, the sense of some helpless melting before a golden force. "I was just telling Whit how I envy your ability — the way you give shots, and don't fold up in surgery and all. I mean you're going to be a great vet, Diane — you really are."

"Why, thank you, Ma'am." Diane laughed and tossed back her hair. She looked surprised and very pleased. "That's not what girls usually envy me for!"

"Well, I could name a couple of other things."

Both Whit and Diane laughed, and he put a protective arm around her. "She's too little to be a vet. She's too beautiful to waste on mere dumb beasts."

"Oh, you!" Diane jerked away. Her whole manner was still lilting, electric with her playful charm, yet her annoyance was plain. "You don't understand a thing about me and never will. Here" — she turned to Tracey — "I was going to ask lover boy to take this medicine up to Dr. B., but you may have the honor."

Doubtfully Tracey accepted the bottle. "Do I dare? I didn't exactly cover myself with glory my last time up there."

"Listen, don't say anything and she won't even notice," Diane advised. "Just stick around, learn what you can — at least till she chases you out. That's the way I got my start."

Scared but breathless with gratitude, Tracey did precisely that. And Dr. Baldwin was so absorbed in what she was doing — a fairly routine spaying job — that she scarcely looked up to see who was handing her things. Not until it was over, and Tracey was carrying the still-limp animal off to the recovery room, did the doctor acknowledge her presence. " Well, Tracey, I see they smuggled you in."

" Yes." Quaking, Tracey came up short. " Everybody else was busy and — " She turned, her face anxious. " I hope I did O.K.! "

" You didn't pull any boners, and you didn't pass out. In fact, I think all patients will survive, including me. Now get on back downstairs where you belong."

Laughing with relief, aglow with appreciation for everyone, Tracey went back to attending mangy dogs.

Suddenly, and rather appallingly, she and Diane became bosom friends. At night they went their separate ways. By day, however, Tracey found herself the unwitting half of a collusion against Whit — two women conspiring together to intrigue and tease and generally deflate the ego of an unsuspecting enemy male. Diane was expert at the game, and at first Tracey found it exciting. To be Diane's confidante. To be the one Diane preferred to work with now, cutting Whit subtly out. To laugh together at the tables, join in sly jokes at his expense.

The men had played jokes on Tracey too, at first. Once they'd convinced her a large alligator had escaped and was hiding in the back seat of an embassy limousine. And she, in her zeal to please, and far more daunted by the liveried chauffeur than a little thing like an alligator, had nearly caused an international incident by trying to slip into the back seat to look. Another time she had almost bitten into a "hot dog" that proved to be the remnants

110

of a brown mutt's severed tail.

But she had been young and gullible: such pranks were but a part of her initiation into the sacred cult. It was something else to see an old hand like Whit taken in, simply because he was so blindly, absurdly in love. It was as if he'd been robbed of his senses. But though Tracey thought wickedly, Goody, now maybe we're getting even! she winced too. She felt guilty and a little scared, as if Diane had her too mesmerized.

"Honestly, did you ever see anybody quite so dumb?" Diane implored, still wiping her eyes from laughing, after Whit had gravely swallowed their story about a nonexistent call from the Republican Party about an elephant they wanted to board. He had even gone out to look over the exercise building for space.

"He's not really dumb," Tracey said. "At least he wasn't until you came."

"I know. That's true — it's just an unfortunate effect I seem to have on men." Diane gave a troubled shrug and flipped her hair back in distress. They were lunching today, for a change, at the corner drugstore. It was flattering to be in the company of a girl so beautiful people kept looking at them. "Poor Whit! I just don't know what to do about him," Diane said, twisting her glass with the hand that wore his big heavy ring.

"Aren't you in love with him?"

"I don't know. Sometimes desperately. But sometimes I can hardly stand him. If he weren't such a slavey, wouldn't show all that disgusting devotion! It's really awfully hard to love a man who insists on throwing himself at your feet like a rug."

"Yes, it must be awful," Tracey sympathized. "I can imagine."

"Tell me what you really think about him?"

"Me?" Tracey gulped. "Well, I'm prejudiced. I think he's — wonderful. He's been awfully good to me — tough on me, but good. I think he's great, and the girl who gets him may have a hard time with him, but she'll still be lucky."

"Why, Tracey, you're blushing!" Diane made a trilling sound with her tongue. "I do believe you've got a crush on him."

"Getting a crush on Whit is practically a reflex action. I've noticed it with almost every girl who gets within ten feet of him. And I've been a lot closer than that for two months now. But nobody's got a chance: he simply doesn't see or hear or want to think about anybody but you."

Diane gave a little shiver, half of despair, half of delight. "I wouldn't be human, especially a human female, if I didn't get a kick out of knowing that. But I wouldn't be honest, either, Tracey, if I didn't tell you it also worries me."

"I suppose. It does put you in a spot if you can't reciprocate. But be nicer to him, won't you? I mean it's too — awful, the way we've both been treating him. Too kind of cruel."

Diane nodded. And solemnly promising themselves that they would reform, they would positively do better, they returned to the hospital.

What's more, Diane spent the afternoon being unusually sweet to Whit. Tracey, feverishly scrubbing kennels again, told herself she was glad. How would it feel, she wondered, to have another girl tell you that a man like Whit was so absolutely dedicated to you that he couldn't even consider anybody else? What girl, even Diane, so lacking in vanity that she wouldn't find him suddenly newly desirable? The first tender excitement was back in

112

their voices; there was a dazzling, yielded look in Diane's eyes. And now that Tracy had deliberately plunged the knife into her own breast, she took such comfort as she could in her suffering. Worse, even worse than the spectacle of Whit's happiness with Diane, was the weak, sorry spectacle of his despair without her.

Tracey polished off the last cage, filled the last pan with fresh drinking water, and went across the courtyard to help lead the dogs back from the runs. Well, at least somebody loves me, she thought lugubriously, as Butch, as usual, planted huge paws on her shoulders and ardently licked her face. "Down, boy, down!" She struggled him playfully to the floor, and led him padding back into the noisy kennel room.

Whit was just trotting down the open steel stairs, and Diane flitting in through the opposite door, when Butch spotted Whit and snarled. The beatific look Whit had been wearing fled. He blanched. "That wretched beast!" he muttered darkly.

Butch, who could sense an insult a mile away, let out a resounding bellow. The whole encounter was so unexpected that Tracey hadn't time to get a tighter hold on the leash. Before she could stop him, Butch had lunged free, and Whit was streaking for the first available refuge — Butch's cage! Diving in, he slammed the door.

It all happened so fast, and such chaos followed, that for a minute there wasn't time to see how funny it was. Then suddenly it was hysterical — seeing Whit so white and mad and shaken, peering out from behind Butch's bars, while the Great Dane barked.

The girls doubled up with laughter; the men, tearing down to share the excitement, slapped their knees. Even Dr. Baldwin, hastening in from her office, stood shaking silently. Then she snapped her fingers, gave a few brisk orders. Butch was subdued and chained, and Whit slunk free.

White with anger, Whit stalked off, while the girls, unable to stop laughing, escaped upstairs.

" It's too — too — awful — when we meant so well! We — tried! "

" I know, but he — Oh, poor Whit! Did you ever see anything so— so — "

They collapsed on the couch. Despite their noble pact, Whit had been violently laid low before their eyes once more.

Chapter 11

TRACEY SWUNG DOWN off the roan gelding she'd been riding, fished in the pockets of her skin-tight old jodhpurs for a last lump of sugar, and patted the whiskery nose that lipped it from her hand. She perched on a fence, watching wistfully as the groom led the horse back to the stables.

" Cheer up, Trace! " Jeff startled her, coming up from the direction of the office, where he'd been settling for their ride. " We'll be back again before too long."

" No, we won't," she said firmly. " Not this summer. I can't let you spend this kind of money. Nine bucks! " she groaned.

He too laughed and mopped his brow. " It does seem pretty fantastic, after riding all day for free back home." He reached up and half lifted, half caught her as, flustered, she tried to scramble down. " It was worth it, though, seeing you ride. You sure you haven't been keeping a couple

114

of horses hidden in a closet someplace all this time? "

" They're about the only animal we didn't try to hide in that apartment house. Poor Mom! "

" Your mother's wonderful, isn't she? And still so pretty too. It's a wonder she didn't marry again."

" She's had plenty of chances," Tracey said as they walked along the shady path to where the Packard was parked. To her embarrassment, Aunt Azalea practically forced it on them every time they went anywhere. The last thing Tracy wanted was for Jeff to get the idea that the women in her family were eager for him to take her out. Sometimes, just to counteract this ghastly impression, she said she was busy or already had a date when he called. " Mom felt it wouldn't be fair to me. Sometimes, though, I wish she had."

" I'm glad she didn't," Jeff said. " I was always in love with her, as a kid. I always intended to grow up and marry her myself someday." They both laughed, as he helped Tracey into the car. " Of course, I'm a big boy now and see how crazy that was. But it's still less of an adjustment, her being pretty much as she was. But best of all is finding you haven't grown up all sophisticated and impossible, finding you haven't changed too much."

" Thanks," said Tracey, not sure whether to be complimented or not. " You've changed, though," she accused. " You're so tall and — grown-up. Your eyes are the same, but your face is different! "

" Sorry." He knocked with a light distress at a high cheekbone. " I'm not satisfied with it, either. I'd sure send it back if I could."

" Oh, Jeff, it's not that! You know what I mean. It's an awfully good-looking face. It's just change that's hard to accept. Even the ranch. Somehow I can't bear to think of its being broken up, and with another couple on it, even

115

a grown-up, married Ricky that I wouldn't know any more, either. Because it's been home to me always, in my mind. I've always dreamed of the day when I could go back."

"I guess it's like Thomas Wolfe said, 'You can't go home again.' Do you know his work? There's never any real going back in time. We have to accept change, in ourselves and other people, and just — go ahead."

"Animals have it a lot easier," Tracey sighed. "They don't worry about all this."

"No, but they miss a lot. Frankly, I can't think of a single cow, horse, or even platypus I'd change places with right now." Jeff reached over to give her a friendly shake. "Since you're so fond of animals, how about stopping at the zoo? We could pick up a sandwich for ourselves, and some peanuts for the elephants, and look around. I'd like to see those hybrid bear cubs."

Tracey was delighted. The zoo was one of her favorite haunts. It was exhilarating to be here with someone as attractive as Jeff, instead of plain old Dud, with whom she usually came. Dudley knew all the scientific names of all the beasts and was practically on speaking terms with them. Feeling as proprietary as if she owned the place, Tracey couldn't resist showing off some of her own knowledge as she led Jeff around.

"Help, I'm too impressed!" Jeff protested, as she explained that Mack, the Siberian crane, was the zoo's oldest known inhabitant and had his own heat lamp in the winter, and that a pair of adjutants, or marabou storks, got along well with zebras but couldn't abide the other birds.

"Well, it's no fair, really," Tracey admitted. "A friend and I come here quite a lot. In fact, we've even discussed going into zoo work someday."

"Isn't a zoo a sort of odd place for a woman vet?"

"Not necessarily. They call on Dr. Baldwin's services

116

every once in a while out here. Of course, she's unusual."
The familiar worshipful light was on her face. "Boy! If I
can just be half as good as she is someday!"

"You really mean it, don't you?" he asked, as they
walked on to where the polar bears were cavorting and
playing to the audience like sly, heavy, clownish old men.
And as Tracey looked at him in surprise, he added, "All
this animal doctor business — it's not just a passing fancy
or a hobby with you?"

"Hobby?" Tracey hooted. "All I know about my future is, it's got to have animals in it. Whether it's in a zoo,
or having a hospital of my own, or a farm, who knows?
But I know the animals are the most important part."

"More important than the people?" Jeff grinned when
they had pitched a few peanuts to the big shaggy white
ham actors and walked on.

"Oh, goodness no — correction! Why, I want to get
married in the worst way. And have children — kids running all over the place, dogs and cats and kids and horses
and — and a wonderful, understanding husband who
wouldn't mind if I got called out in the night to attend a
neighbor's sick cow. Because I'd also like to combine all
this with being a vet." She gazed at him despairingly. "I
guess it all sounds pretty insane."

"No." He steered her around a bevy of Brownie Scouts
and their leaders, who were buying balloons from the sidewalk vendor. "In a way it's kind of sad. Because that last
picture you painted — I can see it so plain — it's the ranch.
Only it's all changed, as I told you, and I won't be there
much longer, not if I go into foreign service."

"You?" She gazed at him, troubled and intrigued. She
didn't know quite what he meant.

"Yes, me. As I said before, Tracey, it's a crazy, mixed-up
world. And not the least crazy part of it is the people,

117

never really recognizing what they want until it's too late. Here I thought it was your mother I missed most all these years and could hardly wait to see. And I come out here and find out it's really you."

"Thanks." It was all Tracey could think to say, she was so overcome. Was he talking about family affection, she wondered, or the romantic kind? She'd had so little experience with the latter. What's more, her own feelings for Jeff had veered so confusingly between both all these years. And if she couldn't make sense of her own emotions, how could she figure out his?

One thing sure, it had been so long since she'd had a compliment even remotely romantic that she decided not to risk it. Better to change the subject than to push her luck too far, find out she was just imagining that thrilling seriousness.

"Would — would you care to go see the gorillas?"

There was no doubt how he felt about Grandma and Aunt Azalea, and Mother, of course. And the two older women were so crazy about Jeff it was downright embarrassing. Aunt Azalea not only offered up the Packard, she tried to press money on Jeff when he was low on funds. While Grandmother, to Tracey's mixed misery and pleasure, invited him to meals. Tracey would arrive home from work, weary, fleabitten, and smelly, and there, looking cool, brown, and relaxed as he sipped limeade on the patio with the old darlings, he'd be.

Torn between delight and dismay, feeling at an awful disadvantage, she'd say something dumb like, "Well, you here again?" and rush off upstairs to shower. Then came the dreadful decision: what to wear? If she put on anything soft and feminine, as she desperately longed to, he might get the idea she was dressing up for him. Rather than let him think she was in on any possible flirtatious conspiracy, she usually settled for Bermudas, or her plainest blouse and skirt. And then, to make doubly sure, she'd be so cryptic at dinner, drop so many hints about the studying they both should be doing, that often he'd leave right after dessert. Then, mad at herself and utterly miserable, Tracey would walk the dogs in the peaceful cemetery. At such times having them with her was the only consolation she could think of for having moved in with her great-aunt.

It was somewhat better when Jeff showed up of his own accord. After nine o'clock, usually, with the argument that his studying was all done. On such nights they would walk over to a restaurant a few blocks away, a romantic basement place with brick walls and sawdust on the old stone floor. The place was all blue shadows and little gold flames from the candles stuck in bottles, and noisy with the music that poured in a plinking rain from an upright piano and the laughter and singing of the college students who hung out here.

Tracey loved the excitement of being there, but she also felt young and insecure. Not that she showed it. She had a brash, determined way about her, a flip, almost careless manner of rising to new situations that gave an impression of ease. But inside she suffered. She felt as if she needed a buffer between these older, more knowing ones, which included Jeff himself. Jeff, who paid her such flattering almost compliments that she didn't know whether or not to believe. Jeff, who wasn't really Jeff any more, but an attractive, thrillingly rugged yet suave young man whose destiny lay not on a ranch in Wyoming but in exotic-sounding foreign embassies.

Sometimes she urged her mother to join them, and, since Jeff too insisted so heartily, Ellen sometimes came. There was a certain comforting reassurance in her mother's presence: Tracey wasn't thrown so completely on her own; it was more like family. On the other hand, Mom was so mature, so confident, so able to talk to Jeff on an adult level. Now Tracey suffered the pangs of feeling left out a little. Also, she found a secret, tormenting pleasure in watching the little attentions Jeff paid her mother — holding her chair or her wrap. Not that he wouldn't do the same things for any woman, but still —

Maybe it wasn't too impossible, she goaded herself. Maybe Jeff actually was in love with her mother! Tracey knew it was preposterous even as she played with the dark fascination of it. Nonetheless there was a perverse satisfaction in pitying herself and acting aloof.

Ellen, sensing this, refused the next time she was asked. " I'm too tired for all that noise and confusion," she claimed, looking up from the dressing table where she was doing her nails. " I'm not as young as I used to be. And in some ways you're not as old."

" What d'you mean? " Tracey gasped.

" You seemed pretty childish the last time we were all together. If you're not mature enough to go places with Jeff, better stick to boys like Dud." And as Tracey stood outraged, her mother reached out her hand. " Don't blame other people for you own deficiencies, Tracey. As I say, if it makes you uncomfortable to be with Jeff in places like that, do something else. But above all, don't shift the blame for your own discomfort on somebody else."

" You don't know what you're talking about! " Tracey retorted, and stormed out. But halfway downstairs she halted, ashamed. It was a struggle, but she got herself in hand and went plunging blindly back. " I was jealous! " she announced, head low. " I'm sorry."

Her mother didn't probe. She just looked at Tracey a minute, then gave her a brief hug. " I can see your point.

120

Jeff's a pretty choice catch. But next time pick on somebody your own size to be jealous of! "

Laughing, Tracey flew down the steep back stairs. Jeff was waiting in the garden, with its tingling smell of herbs and boxwood and moss-grown fountains. Hand in hand, they slipped through the iron gate that led to the cemetery side, and, deftly skirting graves, reached the cobbled street. " It's sneaky, but it's the only way to get out of having to take that old Packard."

" You said it," Jeff laughed. " And it spares me explaining to your aunt that I'd rather spend my own two bucks to buy you a pizza than her fiver to buy you a steak."

" That's another thing." Tracey slowed down for breath. " If I've been kind of ornery at times, it's because I don't want you thinking I enjoy having them run interference for me."

" I know it," he grinned. " I must be a glutton for punishment, I guess. You notice I keep coming back? "

She nodded and flashed him a pert, flirtatious look shamelessly copied from Diane. It worked too: Jeff held her hand in tighter grip. It was a moment of happiness, pure and acute, on the heels of her bout with Mother. The sky was trembling with a soft lavender light. A mockingbird sang from a mimosa tree that splayed its feathery flowers in a pink-and-green fountain whose fragrance stirred the senses. Their faces were both so radiant that a distinguished-looking man walking a collie smiled and bowed to them, bemused.

Jeff opened the blue wooden outer gate that led to the restaurant, and they went down the damp-smelling, cracked stone steps. It was cool inside, and noisy, as they threaded their way among the checkered tablecloths. The air was blue with smoke and alive with the smell of butter and onions. Resolving not to be nervous, Tracey sat

121

down as Jeff pulled back her chair. Mother was right, she realized, wincing. It was despicable to turn on other people because they were more at home than you were in social situations, to act as if your own failings were somehow all their fault. Facing up to that made her feel newly confident. She smiled at Jeff, across the handwritten menu that it was almost hopeless to try to read in the flickering light.

" Well, what'll you have? " he asked expansively, responding to her mood. " The sky's the limit, providing it's not over a dollar and a half."

" How about some lasagna? " she decided, having overheard a very smart-looking girl ordering it the last time. " The salad comes with it for free."

" That's the spirit — sheer, reckless economy." Jeff leaned back, beckoned to the waiter, who bent, pad in hand, the better to hear. " The young lady will have the lasagna. Roquefort dressing on her salad — right? " he asked Tracey. " Russian on mine. Make the lasagna two — " He broke off abruptly, staring toward the door.

Tracey followed his eyes, and her heart came to a dead stop, then began to race. A familiar tall dark figure and a petite silver-blond one were conferring with the head waiter. The restaurant was designed to branch off into several small brick alcoves. Another waiter beckoned, and they headed in his direction. In a minute they would disappear. Should she wave, get their attention, invite, " Come sit with us " ? Or just scrooch down where she was, unnoticed in the candlelight?

Tracey was torn. She longed desperately to show Jeff off. She'd tried to brag about him to Diane, if only to let Diane know there were some romantic complications in her life too. Not that Diane paid much attention: she was one of those people so enthralled in their own affairs that they can't imagine anything interesting happening to you. Against this impulse to vaunt him, however, Tracey felt a sharp flash of reluctance, a kind of mute, defiant, feminine instinct to guard fiercely against losing what she had.

"What's the matter?" Jeff asked.

"Oh, nothing. I—I just thought I saw somebody I knew."

"In this black hole of Calcutta?" He shielded his eyes. "It'd be hard to recognize your own brother in here. But, say, do you see that girl? Look—going into that other room. Did you ever see anybody as beautiful in your life?"

Tracey's heart kept banging away. She took a sip of water. Her throat felt dry. "How do you feel about beautiful girls, Jeff? In general, I mean?"

"Oh, I'm all for 'em. Unfortunately, you don't see many on a Wyoming ranch."

Tracey matched this up with Whit's grim pronouncements, and actually drew a little breath of relief. "Would —you like to meet one right now?"

"You don't mean you know her?"

"For your information that girl and I played nursemaid to a monkey all afternoon. She works at the hospital too — the girl, I mean. The monkey belongs to a biology prof at Maryland U, and is he a bad actor — the monkey, I mean." She was talking fast, talking nonsense to cover up her confusion and distress. She'd changed her mind. Why, oh, why, she wondered now, had she ever opened her big mouth?

Still, she had a queer feeling about it too. After all, Jeff was likely to meet Diane sometime. And just because Whit was so absolutely gaga about the girl it didn't automatically follow that Jeff would be. Having figured this out, she was still glad she had resisted the temptation to call to them. Time enough to get together later, she was thinking. Then they reappeared. And spying Tracey, Whit cried out, " Well, hi! Look who's here! "

Diane's face too lighted up. "Well, hello! They're all filled up in there."

"Oh, sit with us," Tracey urged, almost too cordially. "We've just ordered. Jeff, I want you to meet a couple of friends from the hospital. Diane Osborne and Whit — Mr. Whitney: he won't tell us his first name."

"Wonderful! This is wonderful! Do sit down! " Jeff was on his feet, holding Diane's chair. And she was flipping back her hair with that exquisite little gesture, and making that charming little bird sound of surprise and delight, a kind of whistled trilling that marveled, made it something special, saying: " Jeff. The — big brother from Wyoming? "

Big brother. Suddenly, appallingly too late, Tracey realized that in her stupidity she had used that term once or twice in describing him to Diane. And now he was labeled and tagged. In one deft instant Diane had plucked that label and pinned it on him — a sign that also said in letters bold and blazing that from now on she was free, if she wished, to go after him.

Only she didn't have to. For Jeff was gazing at her as if transfixed. And Diane was humming softly in her throat and gazing back at him in that innocent yet fateful way she had. And you could feel it, like an electric force around the table: her personality, meshed so immutably with her physical loveliness. And that Jeff was utterly, hopelessly captivated. And Whit — you could feel his suffering too, dumb and desperate. And because of it, of feeling so sorry for him, it seemed almost unjust and childish to have any pity left over for yourself.

"Well," Tracey suggested brightly, because it seemed she had to say something to let them know she was still

124

there, "anybody else care to eat? I'm so hungry I could devour Bozo. In fact, I get so mad at him I'd like to, wouldn't you, Diane? The monkey I told you we were taking care of at the hospital," she informed Jeff.

Not that he heard a word. He just kept looking at Diane.

Chapter 12

WHEN TRACEY AWOKE the next morning, she lay testing her own chaotic emotions. Life seemed so hopelessly tangled that she actually twisted this way and that in the bed, as if to work free from its knots. She was jealous of everybody in this little drama now. Let's face it, she thought. Not only of Diane and Whit, but of Jeff!

Last night had been a minor nightmare, one in which even her mother's advice hadn't helped. Because it wasn't merely that they were all older, more socially experienced: it was just that she had had to sit by watching a triangle develop before her very eyes. One in which, most unkindest cut of all, she didn't even figure. An excruciating triangle that involved Jeff, her Jeff, and Whit, her Whit — and Diane. And she didn't know which of the two boys she was the more jealous of, or resented the most, or felt the most wretched for. One thing sure, there had been no role for her but that of a useless, foolishly squeaking extra wheel —

Henry the Eighth chose this minute to land with a furry plop on her face. In her anguish, Tracey flung the big Maltese angrily to the floor. Then, contrite, she sprang out of bed to snatch him up, taking such comfort as she could from his hearty purring as she crushed him close.

"Sorry, old man!" she muttered, stamping toward the

125

shower. "But when you and some other tom are getting ready to tear each other apart for some female, at least you're honest about it. You don't sit politely eating spaghetti!"

Jeff had been strangely silent, walking home. Not until they had reached the recumbent stone cats that guarded Aunt Azalea's house had he come out with it. "Are they engaged?" Just like that, direct and clear.

"Well, I don't really know," she had told him honestly, with sinking soul. "Sometimes they are and sometimes not." She swallowed. "I — I have an impression it's sort of off right now."

"Good!" he said. "Because frankly that's one girl I intend to see more of — if she'll let me." He had taken both Tracey's arms and turned her squarely to face him. "Thanks for introducing her to me."

And then, to add insult to injury, or ecstasy to outrage or something, he had lifted her chin and kissed her! Tracey had been so astonished she'd stepped backward, nearly squashing another in the inevitable cats, which gave out a bloodcurdling shriek and shot between Jeff's legs so fast he nearly fell down.

"Don't mention it!" Tracey had gasped. And beating a fist against her still tingling lips, she had fled.

It still seemed too ludicrous. Ludicrous and incredible and insulting and everything else outrageous she could think of. Calling it a kiss of gratitude, even the friendly kiss of a big brother, didn't take care of it at all. Jeff, who had always seemed so uncomplicated, clear as a mountain stream, had now complicated her own emotions beyond her own imagining.

Just to remember that kiss made her want to laugh and cry and start yelling and throwing things. How dared he? He'd come, in answer to a dream. And he'd given her such

126

happiness these past few weeks, made her almost believe he loved her. Almost, when she was with him, she could forget the mixed joy and despair of her hopeless passion for Whit. But then to kiss her for the first time as a kind of — reward. For him not to kiss her, even once, until the very night he practically told her he was writing her off his list for another girl!

Well, he didn't know what he was getting into, Tracey thought with bitter satisfaction, sitting on the floor to put on her shoes. He was asking for trouble. And not only from Whit, at that. There must be something destructive about Diane's kind of beauty. Look what it had done to Whit. Fastening the twin buttons of her tailored black shirt collar, Tracey stood protesting. No, oh, no! She couldn't stand idly by watching the same thing happen to Jeff!

But how could she prevent it? Nothing she could do or say to any of them, Whit or Diane or Jeff himself, would do any good. They'd think she was jealous — which she was. They'd think she was a stupid, interfering kid.

Much as she dreaded seeing Diane this morning, it was a relief to plunge into the usual chaos at the hospital. With dogs barking, cats howling, telephones ringing, the parrot screeching: "Hey, good lookin', where ya going?" and Bozo rattling the bars of his cage and pitching back his food — carrots, peanuts, and bananas, as fast as you put them in, followed by the complete contents of his water pan — your own feverish feelings were pretty well drowned.

"That ornery ape!" Tracey scolded, spanking at her slopped apron. "Wish they'd ship him back to the jungle."

"Why, Tracey, how can you talk about dear little old Bozo like that?" Diane was twinkling, in a gay mood. She flitted to the cage and began to trill gaily to the monkey, who sprang lightly up, clinging to the bars with one hand, stretching out the other. Diane clasped it, nuzzled her nose toward the pink one, and the two stood chortling and caressing.

"Men — and monkeys," Tracey grinned. "I've got to hand it to you, Diane."

"Speaking of men — " Diane's eyes shone. "That big brother of yours is something! "

"He's something, but it isn't my big brother," Tracey said darkly.

"Oh." Diane stood considering. "Well, look — he called me up later last night, and we must have talked an hour. I hope you don't mind."

"It's a free country." Tracey grimly filled in Bozo's chart. "But what about Whit? "

"He doesn't own me. We're not married, and the way he's been acting, I doubt if we ever will be. He's got to get used to the idea that I'm going out with other people too — I'm going to date other boys."

"You mean Jeff? "

"Yes. In fact tonight. He's taking me to the Carter Barron Amphitheater to see the Royal Canadian Ballet. Listen, Tracey," she said earnestly, and there was a trace of contrition on her face, "if you have any objections — "

"Oh, no, no, no! " Tracey claimed, though she felt hot and sick all over. Jeff had taken her to the big open amphitheater too once, under the stars. They'd used Grandma's book of season tickets and Aunt Azalea's car. They'd sort of trapped him into going, though it had been a glorious evening — a riotous one-man show with a famous Hollywood star.

"Well, good! Because we'll have to hurry up if we're going to get acquainted — he's going back West in two more weeks."

128

" I know."

" I'm glad you're so understanding, Trace. I knew I could count on you. Be nice to Whit for me, will you? Poor Whit! Do what you can to persuade him that this isn't the end of the world or anything. He thinks a lot of you — he really does. He'll listen to you."

" I hadn't noticed it lately," Tracey said shortly. " Not since you came."

" I don't blame you," Diane said with that mild, dazzling, innocent way she had. " I guess I do seem pretty grizzly, lousing things up for you here at the hospital: the — the nice working arrangement or whatever it was you had with Whit. And now asking you to take him off my hands so I can explore the possibilities with your man! " She gave a helpless little shrug. " I guess I'm just a hideous person. Honestly, sometimes I can hardly stand myself."

" Oh, for Pete's sake! " Tracey said angrily, thrown off guard. When the truth is so expertly packaged and handed you so sweetly, it seems graceless not to protest. " You can't help being so beautiful it hurts. If men go around cutting their throats over you, it's not your fault. And there's hardly a girl alive who wouldn't trade places with you! "

And that was the truth too, she realized dazedly, tramping off to change her apron. Not that this made it any easier for a plain, ordinary girl to take.

She had put on a fresh apron and was in the kitchen preparing foods for the special diets, when the commotion broke loose below.

" Help, help! Everybody come help! Bozo's out! "

Tracey shoved the unappetizing mixture she'd been warming to one side and rushed to the stairs. Whit, who'd been in surgery helping Dr. Baldwin crop ears this morning, stuck his head out. Even now, it seemed to Tracey, he wore a stricken, anxious look that had nothing to do with any monkey save himself.

"Don't worry." She felt a sudden helpless compulsion to console him even in this round-about way. "We — I'll catch him, don't you worry."

"Get him before he gets into anything!" Dr. Baldwin yelled from the operating table. "You too, Whit — this can wait. Everybody catch that monkey before he wrecks the place!"

Tracey tore down the open staircase, Whit close behind her. Stirred frantically by any disturbance, every dog in the place was barking at the top of his lungs. Downstairs, people were pointing and dashing madly about, while Bozo scampered over the tops of the upper kennels, then swung lithely to a big central brass lamp fixture, where he sat like a mischievous old man, scolding and gaily rattling the chains and obviously enjoying the consternation.

"Bozo, you bad monkey, you come right down here!" Even Mrs. Phillips had left her desk to rush back. She shook her finger. "Bad monkey! Bad, bad boy!"

"Let me try. Here, Bozo! Come, Bozo, good Bozo, come to Diane." Bozo cocked his head, seemed to consider as Diane went into her series of trills and chirpings.

"It's a push-over now," Whit remarked with an acrid tenderness loud enough for all to hear. "Look, everybody! Watch. See how she can even charm monkeys off lamps!"

Startled, not liking his tone, Diane turned her head, and in a flash Bozo was gone. The hanging fixture lurched, swung back and forth in orbit, as, supple as silk and trigger-quick, the furry, pink-gray figure shot into space. Catching a rafter with one hand, he hung there taunting them; then with deft use of both tail and paws he pro-

130

gressed nimbly to the partition that led to the pharmacy and disappeared.

"The pharmacy, the pharmacy!" Whit yelled. "Catch him quick, before —"

Already they could hear the horrifying sounds of breaking glass. Frantic, falling over one another in their haste, the entire staff of the hospital burst through the door — to be greeted by a barrage of bottles. Whit, who was first, managed to catch a full bottle of alcohol, and duck the next, which broke at his feet.

"Stand back! Everybody stand back!" he ordered. "This character's aim is good. Somebody could get hurt!"

As if to demonstrate, Bozo reached down from his perch atop a glass cabinet, whose door he had simply unlatched, as he had contrived to unlatch his cage, selected another bottle and, eying them, tossed it from hand to hand. Then, as Whit inched determinedly forward, hand outstretched, Bozo leaped to the top of another cabinet. There he reached down and, using the bottle as a hammer smashed in the glass.

"The penicillin!" Tracey screamed. "Watch out! Grab him before he gets into the penicillin!"

But Bozo had already scooped up a fistful of the precious vials, each containing ten c.c. of the drug and each worth about twenty dollars. Grandly abandoning the bottle of mere alcohol, he cracked a tube with his teeth, tasted its contents, spat, and hurled it from him. Tracey made a flying leap to catch the next one. Whit dived floorward after another but missed. Suddenly everybody was in the act, darting wildly about after the reckless rain of tubes.

"That's it! That's the ticket! Don't worry about catching Bozo — just catch that penicillin!" Dr. Baldwin had made her way through and was crisply cheering them on. She

131

looked extremely concerned, but her composure even now was a thrilling thing to witness.

The other work of the hospital came to a standstill as the epic game of catch continued. There was an awful lot of penicillin to be pitched, and Bozo had plenty of time. Furthermore, he was playful and inventive. With one tube clenched between his teeth and one in each hairy fist, he would caper back and forth along the shelves, or swing from the chandelier by his tail. All anybody could do was stand by, nervously alert for the pitch. And just when they'd think he was tiring, ready perhaps to give up, and someone would creep cautiously toward the cupboards, he would furiously heave what he had and soar back for a fresh supply.

Meanwhile, Mrs. Phillips returned to the office to take phone calls and calm the clients. Dr. Baldwin went on attending to the other animals single-handed.

"Don't worry," she said patiently. "Bozo will be hungry enough to quit soon, or the penicillin will give out."

"It's about given out now," Tracey was grateful to report. "But we've saved at least half of it, maybe more."

"Good girl! We've got a good staff. Teamwork — that's the main thing in a place like this." She gave Tracey a long, searching look, said cryptically, "At least this proves we all can play ball together if we try."

At that moment, flushed, perspiring, but triumphant, Whit appeared. And riding his shoulder as innocent as a baby was the furry demon.

"Praise and hallelujah!" Dr. Baldwin gave a chuckling shout and threw up her hands. "To what do we owe this heavenly vision?"

"He ran out of ammunition. Also, if he's anything like the rest of us, he's starved."

"I assure you he bears a striking resemblance to the

rest of you at times!" the doctor said with dry good humor. "Come here, you simian so-and-so. What d'you mean by bringing us to rack and ruin like that?"

For answer, Bozo began to chatter sweetly, and cupping the doctor's cheeks with his paws, pursed his lips and tried to bestow a kiss. "Now no soft soap! Cut that out! You go into a maximum security cage with a double lock. Where he should have been put in the first place," Dr. Baldwin added and, turning to them, said: "I'm not going to ask who's responsible for not seeing to it that he was. All I can say is: this has been a very expensive lesson for all of us. And it had better not happen again."

Tracey's heart began to beat wildly. Her knees shook and her face flushed. She had this terrible talent for looking guilty no matter what. But searching her conscience, she was infinitely thankful to discover that she hadn't had a thing to do with it. Who, then? Whit, she distinctly remembered, had been helping Dr. Baldwin treat an emergency the afternoon Bozo came in. That left only one of the men — or Diane. And surely old hands like Jake or Bert would have known better. No one offered an explanation.

Tracey could not, however, bring herself to proclaim her innocence. She stood there looking as much a criminal, she knew, as if she had personally helped Bozo execute his escape.

"What's become of Jeff?" Aunt Azalea fretted a few nights later. "I declare I miss that boy. You two have a falling out?"

Before Tracey, who was feeding the cats, could answer, Grandmother called out through the open French doors: "No, they didn't. I specifically asked him that last night when I invited him for Sunday dinner. He's busy studying for his final exams."

133

"Gam!" Tracey groaned. "You don't mean you called him, after I definitely asked you not to?" She got up, picking her way through the swarm of Persians, Siamese, tigers, tortoise shells, and just plain alley cats, which were daintily lapping and nibbling from the bowls lined up on the red stone side porch.

"Dear me, did you?" Her grandmother stood looking queenly and confused and exasperating in the evening light. She shook her white head. "Yes, I do believe I remember now. Dearie me-oh-my! I get more forgetful every day I live. Well, no matter," she tried to appease both her granddaughter and her own conscience, "since he couldn't accept. The exams, as I believe I said?"

"Exams or not, it does matter!" Tracey cried out. "A girl has her pride. It's too — too degrading to have other people trying to rope a boy in!"

"Jeff? Why, nonsense," Aunt Azalea sided with her sister. "He's practically part of the family. You and your mother have said so, both of you. And Jeff himself has said over and over that's what he'd like to be."

"Well, he won't be saying it any more, thanks to both of you!"

It was rude; it was talking back to her elders, which she'd been taught never to do. Well, she couldn't help it. And to keep from saying any more, she fled.

Safely in her own room, Tracey grabbed one of the thick, carved black-walnut posters of the canopied bed and shook it as furiously as Bozo had been shaking his bars when she had left the hospital. Then she flung herself down and wept. Now in addition to her embarrassment and disappointment and loneliness and jealousy, she must support the added anguish of her own self-accusations. Bungling and mistaken though the old dears were, they meant well. She had no right to attack them like that.

134

To — to make them responsible because she'd lost Jeff to another girl.

Even without their interference, she couldn't have held him. And again Mother's admonition struck home so hard it stung: "Don't blame other people for your own deficiencies."

All the same — Tracy sat up, wiping her eyes on a corner of the spread — she was infinitely glad she'd never brought Whit home to meet them. Not, she recalled miserably, that she'd have the nerve to ask him now, anyway.

The drama, the sense of romantic excitement that had heightened the tempo of the hospital with the arrival of Diane, was fulfilling its promise. The news that Diane was dating somebody else had spread like wildfire. And, naturally, with that curiosity with which the people most afflicted by catastrophe are regarded, all eyes were on Whit.

Diane herself, people paid less attention to. Maybe because people envy and sometimes even resent a little anyone who is so obviously, ecstatically in the throes of a new love. Her face, already so beautiful, was almost enchanted. Tracey could scarcely bear to see her so — don't look, don't look! Her bird trillings and hummings sang of delights too sweet to share. Except when it could not be avoided, the girls no longer worked side by side, and no longer slipped off for lunch. Even the men were a little uneasy in the face of this new development. They left Diane alone, making their wry, amused speculations to one another, and shaking their heads and grinning, "Poor Whit."

No, it was Whit who really interested them. You could feel them watching him with a mixture of pity and subtle male gloating, to see how he was bearing up. And, all things considered, he was bearing up a lot better than Tracey had feared he would.

At least, thank heaven, he had stopped that sickening, doglike trailing around after Diane. He was furiously avoiding her, in fact. Whenever she entered a room his jaw would jut, his eyes begin to smoulder, and he'd turn on his heel, if possible, and leave. Of course there were countless occasions when it wasn't possible — they all had to work together. But Dr. Baldwin, who kept such a keen if quiet eye on all of them, who managed the hectic affairs of the hospital with such a firm and facile hand, was able to keep Diane at her side a good deal.

So that now, again, it was Whit and Tracey who worked together at the tables. And you might as well draw such doleful comfort from it as you could. That Whit was suffering was plain. Tracey could feel the throb of it like her own wound, as they conferred on cases, gave shots, and treated the skin troubles in the afternoon. Yet, perversely, she was almost grateful to that suffering for restoring him, at least a little bit, to the Whit she first had known — terse, sardonic, critical, quick to bawl her out.

"No, no, not that bottle, you idiot! Bring me the Nickathol B. This mutt gets intravenous feeding — won't you ever *learn?*"

"I'm sorry." Tracey dashed off to correct her mistake.

"*I'm* sorry, you mean," Whit said tightly, on her return. "It's not fair making you my whipping boy."

"I don't mind," she told him, wet-eyed but determinedly grinning.

"Well, you should," he snapped. "Listen! Don't make my mistakes, Don't grovel before — anybody, no matter what. Don't ever fall for anybody hard enough to lose your self-respect."

"What're you driving at?" she flared. "You — if you think for one minute I'm sucker enough to — to have any designs on you!"

136

"That's the spirit," he laughed, and gripped her shoulder. "Tell me off, don't take any nonsense, never crawl! It's no good," he said grimly. "Just — no good, letting anybody alive get that kind of hold over you."

"I'm glad you're finally seeing it," she dared breathlessly. "Frankly, I was more worried about you, Whit, before. It's tough to see you so hurt, but it's encouraging to see you so mad again. It's — well, it's more like old times! "

He threw back his head and laughed for the first time in weeks. "You're a good kid, Florence. You're the one who should be mad — don't you realize that? After all, it's your boy friend."

"Oh, I am," Tracey said honestly, lifting the dog from the table and standing there a minute holding him in her arms. "I'm furious. Jeff was my one big interest this summer — he was all I had, not counting Dud. And it seems so unfair that I had to lose him to somebody who already had you! "

Too late she caught herself, plunged on. "But I don't dare ask myself what she's got that I haven't got. The answer's too awful — she's got everything! And while I'm not exactly mad at her for having it — after all, she can't help it, and boy! wouldn't I like to have some of it though? — I'm still mad at everybody involved! "

Oh, it was hopeless! Just too hopeless. Every time they were together she trapped herself, betrayed in a hundred ways, how incurably crazy about him she was.

Chapter 13

AT LAST SHE WAS giving shots. Whit had started her off with rabies injections, showing her how to inject the serum intramuscularly. And after that he taught her how to give shots subcutaneously, which meant right underneath the skin. It was too awful to have him stand there supervising — necessary and sweet but awful. Her knees felt frostbitten: she had to brace them against the table. She managed to keep her fingers steady through sheer will power, but she felt the dire contrast between their clumsiness and Diane's deft touch.

No dog likes it when he's jabbed with a needle, even by an expert. Careful as she was, Tracey was bitten several times. But with Whit there to swab on the stinging antiseptic, it didn't matter. Battle scars, Tracey sometimes thought, surveying her hands, and she felt a kind of glory. How much Whit had taught her this summer! And however painful the lessons, she would treasure every one of them.

"I suppose, under the circumstances," she told Dudley, "I ought to be grateful to Diane. If she hadn't taken Jeff away from me, I wouldn't have Whit back again. Not," she added disconsolately, "that you can call this really having him. But at least it's something, this — this temporary respite from seeing him drooling over her."

"I can't understand it," Dud sighed, stroking Henry the Eighth, who had sprung down from his perch on a gargoyle atop the patio wall. "Two guys in their right minds, I presume, and neither one of them really appreciating a girl like you."

138

"Oh, they appreciate me all right," Tracey protested. "But there's a big difference between being appreciated and being gone on, crazy over, well — nuts about."

"Yeah, yeah, yeah, I see your point. But appreciation's a long-time thing, Trace. Being, nuts, crazy, and all that jazz is — well, that's temporary."

"Not necessarily. Not with a girl like Diane. She's the kind men don't get over. Look at Whit — he's been crazy about her for two years now. In fact, I doubt if he ever will recover, no matter how he acts. That's what's so discouraging about it."

"I guess that puts you in the nuts-about-him class!"

"I guess it does," she admitted helplessly. "But I also appreciate him. You can be both," she said. "Maybe that's what love is. Not only the excitement, the — mad passion sort of flare, but the appreciation. Really admiring what another person's like — his knowledge, his ambition, his basic qualities."

"But I thought this Whit was also a stinker. You've said so yourself."

"Well, yes. He can be pretty awful. Ornery. And he's too moody and a lot of things I don't like much. But you — if you really appreciate somebody," she insisted, "you can put up with his dark side. You can take the bad along with the good."

Dud got up, stretched, yawned, and took her hand in fervent grip. "Sounds like love, Trace."

"I suppose so," she said miserably. "But I'd rather love somebody who doesn't love me than not — be in love at all!"

"Yeah, you said it. Boy! I know exactly what you mean."

"You!" she gasped, and regarded him large-eyed.

" Don't tell me you're carrying a torch for some mysterious woman! "

" Why not? I'm human. I'm not entirely preoccupied with the prevention and cure of leukemia in white rats."

" Of course you're not. And I'll tell her so too, if you'll let me. I'll tell her she doesn't appreciate you the way she should."

" Oh, she appreciates me all right. Only it's like you said — with a girl there's a big difference between appreciation and the grand blast."

The way he was looking at her made her heart melt. " Oh, Dud, no! " she exclaimed, flattered but upset. " Not me. Don't tell me you — you're basing your little case history on me. We know each other too well for that."

" Maybe so. Maybe no. All I know is, like you said, I'd rather be miserable with you than happy with somebody else."

" Do I make you miserable? " she asked contritely.

" Yeah, when I see you so miserable over those other guys. Not that I don't want you telling me about them," he added hurriedly. " I'm honored. I'd like to be able to do something to patch it up for you, so you won't hurt like that. It's queer but when you hurt, I hurt too."

" Don't I know how that is, though! " she cried. " Oh, dear! Life is so mixed up. Why don't the right people ever love the right people? " she demanded. " Honestly, you'd think there'd be a better way of managing things."

" Yeah, you sure would."

" But you're wrong, Dud — you must be wrong about me. Why, as I said before, we know each other too well. We — well, appreciate each other too much. You can't honestly stand there and tell me you've felt the grand blast! "

" Maybe not, but that's no sign. At least not for a man it

140

isn't necessarily. At least not for me."

He gave her a chaste kiss then, and she walked down to the gate with him and watched him climb glumly into his car. She was quite touched. It was thrilling to know that Dud loved her, even when she couldn't return the compliment. It gave her a sense of significance and power. Poor Dud! Bless his heart. She felt grateful to him in an enthralled way, and yet sorry, deeply sorry, for him too.

The feeling brought her up short. How ghastly, how perfectly ghastly if Whit felt the same sense of pity and importance when it came to her! She would have to throw up her defenses afresh, she realized, guard more firmly than ever against the very thing Whit had warned her about: " Letting anybody alive get that kind of hold over you."

Dr. Baldwin came up to the kennel where Tracey was watching the shaggy, panting dog. " How's Cookie doing? "

" She's been tearing up the paper I put in her cage. It looks as if it shouldn't be too long now."

" The sac hasn't broken, has it? "

" Not yet. Her temperature's down, though."

The doctor consulted the chart, then her watch. " Well, look, I'm supposed to address a dinner meeting of the Veterinary Association tonight. I ought to be on my way now — " Hope sprang high in Tracey's breast, the doctor read its echo in her eyes. " How'd you like to play stork? "

Tracey gazed at her in a soft excitement. " Could I? "

" It'll mean staying overtime."

" That doesn't matter."

" I guess you know what to do — you've helped the rest of us often enough. Some hospitals let the mother do all the work, but here we believe in getting them breathing fast. Just take the puppies when they come and snip the cord and remove the sac. You don't have to tie the cord unless the dog's a bleeder, and Cookie isn't. Call the night man if you need any help, and Whit will look in later."

"We'll be O.K., won't we, girl?" Tracey reached in to pat the dog. It was a crossbreed, part Spitz — you could tell that from the fluffy white hair but short-legged like a dachs, with an odd, sharp terrier shape to its nose. A curious, almost comical-looking dog. But somebody loved it: its owner loved it and had brought it in to have this litter delivered.

Above all, right now, it was a female, and Tracey's heart went out to it. "Good girl, good girl," she kept repeating gently as the dog lifted eyes that were disturbed, faintly anxious, pleading, yet wise with some ancient wisdom. And the little bitch responded: how loving she was, nuzzling and sniffing and licking Tracey's hand!

Love, that was the main thing. Whether woman or dog, you needed someone to love you at a time like this. A great surge of affection flowed through Tracey, as if she had touched the very core of compassion. "You'll do all right now, hear? Don't you worry, baby! I'll be right with you."

Dr. Baldwin emerged from her office again, zipping shut her big handsome leather bag, pulling on her scalloped little gloves. "How do I look? Is my hem straight? I'll be standing up behind a table, thank goodness, but it always gives you confidence to know you're not coming apart someplace, especially when you're talking to a bunch of men."

Tracey was almost as honored by this request as she was by the chance to attend the dog. "Oh, yes — yes, you look marvelous," she said "I can't find a thing wrong!"

"Thank you, Tracey. Take down this number — it's where we'll be meeting. Not that you'll need it. Cookie's an old hand at this business — she's had several litters, every one of them mongrels, of course, but fine little dogs. She's a good natural mother — you've got nothing to worry about at all."

"Oh, I'm sure I haven't. And you haven't either," Tracey reassured her. "Everything's under control here, and you'll make those men sit up and beg!"

The doctor laughed and went off looking small and trim.

Mrs. Phillips poked her head in as she left. "How you doing, honey? Here're a couple of magazines I thought you might like while you're waiting." She looked small and warm and motherly, in her print dress, with her white crocheted stole across her shoulders. "Mr. Phillips is taking me to O'Donnell's for a seafood dinner tonight. I didn't tell anybody, but it's our anniversary. We'll stop by later, if you'd like."

"Thanks, that would be nice, but really you needn't bother," Tracey said.

She wanted to be alone. To do it herself. She wished everybody didn't think it necessary to give her all this support. Still, how wonderfully good everyone was being! How kind and considerate! There was something about birth that did that to people, she realized. New life coming into the world. And if it were that way with animals, what must it be like with human beings? The love that accompanied the coming of a baby must be absolutely overwhelming.

You missed a lot, being an only child. She'd never been around a new baby; she wished she could sometime. Her senses yearned.

Tracey pulled up a chair, tried to settle down with *Vogue*. But the sac broke just then, and she got busy with towels. Now it was beginning, really beginning! "Atta girl," she kept encouraging. "You're on your way now, girl."

Still it would be about forty-five minutes before the first puppy appeared. At least that's the way the timing usually went. Tracey was vaguely hungry, and she thought about the sandwich upstairs left over from lunch. But she could not bring herself to leave long enough to get it. Everything was in readiness now: The box with its blankets to receive the puppies, in case the mother rolled on them or otherwise hurt them between deliveries. The neat little roll of tools from the sterilizer. She opened it and gazed at them in fond delight. The hemostats for clamping the cord, the sterile scissors. They gave her a sense of power and authority — and humility. Someday she would reach for such instruments as casually and confidently as Dr. Baldwin. Now they were like shining treasures to be touched with care, regarded with awed respect.

The dog had crouched down in a corner of the kennel now. The panting was intensified. She sounded like The Little Engine That Could chuffing up the mountain. Tracey suddenly remembered the childhood story: "I think I can, I think I can, I think I can!"

Tracey's magazine dropped to the floor. "Of course you can," she murmured. "Of course you can, honey." And even as she stood, enrapt, the first puppy was born.

In a sudden burst of happy confidence, Tracey snipped the cord. Almost no blood, thank goodness! She wouldn't have to tie the cord. "Good girl, good girl," she kept crooning, half to the mother, half to the tiny bundle in her hands. How light and hot it was, barely a scrap of flesh, but living, but living! "Now don't worry," she told the anxious mother. "Your baby'll be safe, won't you, sweetheart?" And still crooning and shaken with delight, she

144

carried it off to the box that was all ready, snug as an incubator, with hot water bottles.

The mother was resting when she returned. Tracey went to the wall tap and ran fresh water into her dish. Thirsty from her labors, the dog lapped up every drop and lifted eyes that were now alert, almost mischievous with some request. Puzzled, Tracey gazed back. "Now what? What're you trying to tell me? Oh, I'll bet I know — your Pepsi!"

"She just loves it," the owner had said, and Dr. Baldwin had agreed that it was all right for her to have it. Laughing to herself, Tracey flew off to the refregerator to get a cold bottle.

The dog was so delighted she rose and wagged her tail, and for a second Tracey had the disappointed fear that one puppy might be all she was going to have. After she had slurped down the first dish of cola, however, she began to whine, and in a few minutes the second puppy came.

The first had been jet black, though Tracey had been too preoccupied to notice. The second was white, with black circles around the eyes, and she fell in love with it at once. The third was already en route by the time she returned from bedding down the second. There was a long wait after that, during which time Cookie got away with another long draught of her favorite drink, and Tracey decided to risk getting one for herself.

"Mind if I join you?" she asked, settling down once again on the chair.

She had just uncapped the bottle when the door opened, and Whit peered in. "Well, Florence, how we doing?"

"Oh — Whit!" She wished, awfully, that he could have arrived at a more dignified, more dramatic moment. It was too sort of flippant to be caught tippling from a Coke bottle, when actually she had been so moved.

145

"We — were just having a Pepsi, Cookie and I. The doctor said to give her some if she wanted it. And she's earned it, haven't you, girl?" Tracey looked up, eyes shining. "She's already had three."

"Pepsies or puppies?"

"Puppies, of course," she told him, flustered. "And, Whit, they're just precious. Come look!"

He followed her to the box where the little newcomers to life were nuzzling blindly and emitting faint, bleating cries. "Aren't they just — just — the most?"

"The ugliest bunch of little mutts I ever saw."

"Don't talk about my family like that!" she told him indignantly.

"Sorry, little Mother. Think she's got any more on the line?"

"Well, I'm not sure. You can tell about that better than I."

They returned to the kennel, where his long, expert hands prodded gently. Then he capped his finger, did an internal. "Yeah, I bet you another Coke she'll turn out at least three more. Feel right here — and here. Want to take me up on it?"

"Not a bet. Get yourself a Coke, but let's not bet on this, Whit, please. I mean — it means too much to me." She was surprised at the shy intensity of her voice, and so was he.

"O.K., sure," he said, and gazed at her a long instant, his eyes searching and tender, though his mouth went down at the corners in its amused, ironic little twist. "Pepsies between puppies!" He laughed shortly and stood jingling his keys. "Now I've heard everything. Listen, Florence, I'm going upstairs to chew the fat with Jake until the night man comes on. I can see I'm not needed around here."

146

"Whit, you're welcome but, that's right, not needed," she told him. "Thanks for letting this be all mine."

One by one the puppies continued to be born. Cookie was quieter now, tired and resting longer between the bringing forth of each new life. It was nearly ten o'clock before the sixth one emerged.

Tracey was tired too with a beautiful weariness. She felt in communion with the dog, which lay panting softly in a light sleep. She felt as if she too had accomplished some natural but marvelous thing. Six puppies! What a good big bouncing litter, she thought, in a little burst of reflected glory. And even as she was congratulating herself as well as the mother, the dog roused and two more were born in quick succession.

Eight! Tracey mopped her face. She laughed. She wanted to shout aloud, and did so. "Whit! Hey, Whit, Jake, somebody — bring me another box, we've got too many occupants for this hotel!"

"Well, I'll be —" Whit came bounding down the stairs in his lithe, graceful way, and behind him Jake, chewing his pipe.

"Some vet you are," she kidded joyously. "I should've taken you up on that bet!"

"Well, live 'n learn," Whit acknowledged merrily. "Six was all I could scout out. The other two must've been high."

"That surely must be all. See if you think she's going to have any more, or if it's safe to put them back in with her now."

"Sure you trust me?" Whit grinned, examining the dog. "Yeah, she's had all the family she's going to have tonight."

"Good. These poor little tykes can use something to eat, can't you, boys?" Tracey bent over them. "Sorry din-

147

ner's late, you poor little rascals — you must be starved."

"Wait." Jake put out a big hairy hand, gentle but restraining. "Ain't no sense doing that, Tracey. Ain't no sense at all."

Tracey paused, two squirming puppies already hot in her hands. Shocked, she looked from one face to the other. "Why not?" she demanded, and when they did not answer, "But of course there's sense to it!" A sharp chill of protest pierced her. Something was wrong, she could feel it, sense it, almost smell it, as an animal scents danger. "They've got to be introduced to their mother right away!"

Scowling, Jake looked helplessly at Whit, who bit his underlip. "Not when they're not going to know their mother, Tracey," he said crisply. "They'll only drain her of milk and strength that she's going to need."

"But she's got to nurse them in order for them to live! She's got — " Her voice broke off. Still clutching the puppies, she stood staring at them. "What're you trying to tell me?" she cried furiously. "That it was all for nothing? That — that she went through all that for — *nothing!* That my first puppies — "

"They've got to be destroyed, Tracey. Dr. Baldwin must've forgotten to make that clear. Or maybe she thought you knew the facts of the case. The owner doesn't want to keep more than one of them. She told us to get rid of all of them except one good, healthy male."

"But that's not fair!" Tracey heard herself cry out. She held the puppies protectively tighter, and her eyes — she couldn't help it — were blind with tears. "They're alive now. And they've only been alive such a little while!"

"Yeah, yeah, yeah — " Jake's big rough hand was on her shaking shoulder. "Take it easy now, you want to be a vet, don'tcha? You gotta get used to facing these things."

148

"It's really better, Trace," Whit was reasoning. Gently but firmly, he took the two small dogs she held. "You know as well as I do it's a lot more unfair to keep animals alive that nobody wants."

"But *I* want them!" she burst out recklessly. "They're my puppies! I want them all! I'll take them home!"

Still scowling but faintly smiling, Jake shook his head. Whit said sternly: "Now listen here, kid! Cut out this monkey business or I'll tell Dr. Baldwin to demote you to deticking and flea detective. A vet's got to be sympathetic, sure, but, just as important, he's got to be objective. If you're going to go bawling your head off over every mutt that comes your way, you're in the wrong business, and you'd better find it out right now!"

"I'm — sorry," she whispered, fighting for control.

"If I was inclined to be real tough, I'd make you drown 'em yourself. Maybe I ought to. If dames are going to go into this profession they shouldn't expect favors. But since this is your first litter, I'll take 'em away." Roughly, as if fighting his own emotions, Whit caught up the box.

"Wait —" Jake cleared his throat. "What about the owner's male?"

"That's right. Listen, Trace, tell you what — we'll let you pick him out."

Tracey gasped. She stood gazing at the whimpering cargo. For one awful instant she was tempted to refuse. It was too terrible a decision. To have helped these tiny creatures come into the world in the first place, and now to be handed the power of life or death over them! Yet she knew, every instinct told her, that she too was on trial. In the eyes of Whit and Jake she would be found unworthy of the calling she longed to follow if she failed.

Her fists knotted. Her protesting eyes went bleakly from one quivering, pulsing, hot little life-hungry being to another. She forced herself to take them up one by one, weighing, examining. Finally, decisively, she lifted the black-and-white one and without a word turned away. She was busy cuddling it up against its mother as the two men went out the back door.

It didn't take long. In about ten minutes she heard the familiar step on the cement floor. Struggling to keep her face composed, detached, indifferent, Tracey turned to Whit — and gasped once more.

For his hands were not empty. Whit, the cold, the curt young man, impatient with mistakes or weakness or tears, held something wrapped in a towel. He gazed at her half apologetically an instant before holding it out to her.

"He was so — little," he said. "And it seemed to me he was the one you had the hardest time putting back. I figure if he gets plenty of milk, as he ought to without all that competition — "

"Whit, Whit!" Shakily she took it. It was, she remembered vividly, the first one, the black one. "Baby, my first baby," she whispered to it. "Eat now, eat up, my darling — you've waited so long."

"He's not the only one that oughta be hungry," Whit said as the puppy burrowed into its mother's side and began vigorously to nurse. "I bet you haven't had dinner, and neither have I. How about a hamburger someplace?"

"Do I dare leave?"

"Sure. Jake says he'll do any puppy-sitting necessary until the night man gets here. Boy! Are you a mess! Go on up and wash now and put your lipstick on."

Laughing but still wanting to cry, Tracey flew upstairs. She did look a mess: her hair was a blond explosion, and her face was streaked, and the apron she'd been wearing couldn't have been worse. Recklessly, she tore it off, began to make repairs.

150

The new little family was asleep when she returned. "Night now. Be good," she told them and turned to Whit, who was smiling at her with the fondest, sweetest, most protective and glorious smile she'd ever seen on his face.

"Florence!" he chuckled, half to himself. "Little old Mummy Florrie that wants to be a vet and yet raise sixteen kids and live on a farm!"

She didn't understand him, this strange unpredictable man, and she guessed she never would. All she knew was it was wonderful — the brusque, half-mocking way he caught her hand and stuck it resolutely through his arm as they went out onto the white, shining streets.

Chapter 14

How FAST it was going now: the whole golden summer, so lazy, so luxuriantly stretching out before you a few weeks back, seemed to be packing up its bags to dash swiftly away. Here and there a maple tree brandished a scarlet leaf, like a small signal flag. Now and then as you walked in the cemetery or led the dogs along the cobbled streets, leaves would coast down to lie like little warnings at your feet. Uncertainty, a feeling of impending departure, was everywhere — in the tangy-smelling Georgetown gardens gaudy with late-burning flowers, in the windows of smart shops displaying luggage and nubby, tweedy college clothes in the burnished colors of fall.

After much discussion, Tracey had enrolled for her senior year at Western, the Georgetown high school nearest her aunt's. For one thing, it would be hopeless to try to find another apartment in their old neighborhood, particularly one that would welcome a cat, two dogs, and a puppy as yet untrained. And while it seemed a pity not to be graduated with the friends she had grown up with, as Tracey explained to her mother: "You know we never had much in common. And working at the hospital with older people this summer — well, I've grown up so much I'm afraid now we'd have even less. Also, since I'm going to keep on helping Dr. Baldwin, it's so much easier to be close like this."

The fact that the doctor had asked her to continue evenings and Saturdays filled her with tremendous satisfaction. She had made good! Despite her many blunders, Dr. Baldwin considered her, Tracey Temple, of such value that she had even raised her pay. Equally important, the doctor lent Tracey books from her library, and in her patient, tactful, unobtrusive way, continued to improve her practical education in the field where so few girls got the breaks.

That was the main thing, Tracey reminded herself, clipping along to work the morning of the farewell party for Diane, who was going back to Iowa State. That compensated for every minute of personal anguish suffered because of mere — people. To have a purpose in life. To know what you really wanted, and be given an opportunity while you were so young to work under the astute eye of an expert in that field.

And Mom, bless her heart, was wrong. "I wonder," her mother had said reflectively only the other night, " I wonder how different your life might have been if your father had lived and I'd been able to stay home and mother you. If we'd had other children, or if I'd married again, given you brothers and sisters. I wonder if you'd have turned to animals for companionship the way you have, to a point of actually wanting to make a lifework of them."

152

It wouldn't have made any difference, Tracey was convinced. She had always been mad for animals, even back on the ranch among all those boys. Nothing could have changed that, she believed, no matter what the other circumstances of her childhood might have been.

Even as her thoughts flashed back to the ranch, her eyes encountered a tall, attractive, bronzed figure just emerging from a corner bookstore. Jeff! There was no avoiding him, and though her heart banged sickeningly, and nervous chills assailed her, she was glad to discover that she didn't want to.

"Well, speak of the devil," she exclaimed. "Or to be more accurate, think of him."

"Tracey! I was just thinking about you too. Got time for a cup of coffee?"

"I'm afraid not. Mrs. Phillips is sick today, and the place will be a madhouse. Why don't you walk along with me?"

"Afraid I can't. Listen, I'll see you tonight, though, at the party for Diane."

"Yeah. It should be a kind of going-away party for you too, I guess. When do you leave?"

"Sunday. And I definitely want to get over to see all of you before then. If I'm still welcome," he added with a doubtful grin.

"You know you're welcome, Jeff," she said. "Nothing could change that. Say, why don't you come for dinner tomorrow night?"

"Could I? That'd be great. Listen, Trace —" He kicked the curb, his blue eyes thoughtful. "I do hope you understand about Diane."

"Boy! Do I!" she was happy to hear her own voice exclaiming without recrimination. But then with things going so swimmingly between her and Whit now, why

153

should she hold a grudge? " Things like that just happen. And as long as everybody's young and free to make choices, well, nobody else should get in the way. Well, I'll be late if I don't scram."

Renunciation speech number nine, she thought wryly, scurrying past him. But she felt a queer, exalted glow. Despite her watery knees and whamming pulses for fear of being too soupy or curt or something and lousing the whole thing up, she'd struck exactly the right note of friendly interest, shed the air of honest well-wishing that now, she realized, she actually felt for both him and Diane. Goody for our side! she thought. You're really getting the hang of living when you can meet unexpected tests like that and come off without making a fool of yourself. Of course, the secret but cozy and comforting knowledge bore in on her: it wouldn't have been quite so easy if she and Whit weren't hitting it off with such promise.

The hospital was indeed a madhouse this morning. If the absence of one person in such an institution could throw things so out of gear, Tracey wondered what it would be like after Diane left. Or if, heaven forbid, Whit himself should ever actually leave! Though that possibility was too ghastly even to consider: she dismissed it firmly from her thoughts as she dashed from kennel to kennel, or back to the tables, or out to grab the frantically ringing phone.

One thing sure, nothing could upset Dr. Baldwin. How supremely calm she was even when they got the emergency case toward noon! A big German shepherd had been hit by a car. He had to be operated on at once, and Whit had to come out of the rather mystifying huddle he was having with Diane for a change and help. This left them even more shorthanded downstairs. It was midafternoon before, tired, dirty, but keenly stimulated, Tracey

154

could even slip up to the lounge to wash her hands and grab a bite of lunch. To her surprise and sharp dismay, Whit and Diane were just rising from the studio couch. Whit, who had seemed so blessedly relaxed lately, wore his old dark, tense look. Diane's face, however, was glowing with that fateful, mischievous innocence that simply boded no good.

"I guess you'll feel pretty lucky to get out of this place, Diane," Tracey said.

"I'll say!" Diane was twinkling, filled with a vast, secretive, gay benevolence. "College ought to seem really peaceful after this."

Still puzzled, but telling herself not to be silly, Tracey unwrapped her sandwiches. She kept hoping Whit would come back, even this late, and prepare his usual offering — black coffee. That silent gesture had always had a miraculous way of making everything seem all right. Of course, running off schedule like this, it was too much to expect. Gamely she made herself some instant and sat sipping it. And through sheer will power and the effect of the nourishment, her spirits revived.

Her thoughts sprang eagerly forward to the cozy times she and Whit would have again. It was awful, maybe, to want to be rid of Diane; she felt a little guilty about it and even missed her already in an odd, aching way — that loveliness! And yet there was no denying what a relief it would be to be spared that competition. And it would be fun to help Dr. Baldwin straighten out, get everything back on some smoothly running plan.

Feeling reinvigorated and efficient, ready for almost anything, Tracey returned to her duties. By some miracle, things were once more under control. Whit and Diane were busy wrapping the paws of a poor little fox terrier suffering from eczema. The victim looked both comical and pathetic as he kept trying to prevent their ministrations. The men were beginning to exercise the other animals, and Dr. Baldwin was about to start her late-afternoon office hours.

"Look, Diane — would you rather I did that while you took over out front?" Tracey asked, for skin cases were one thing Diane had never liked and got out of as much as she could.

"No, thanks. We're almost through, aren't we, Whit?" Diane flashed him one of her dazzling, almost caressing looks. But on the heels of the very pain that smote Tracey came a flash of understanding. Diane was simply in an engaging mood on this her last day — spilling love and favor on everyone as a final gift! The relief of this rationalization made Tracey almost shout.

Diane turned the radiance in her direction. "Why don't you go out and try to keep the customers at bay?"

Tracey took her place behind the desk. "Yes, Mrs. Rayburn, Ginger is doing much better. We think he may be able to go home tomorrow. . . . Name and telephone number, please. Dog's name, please. And what seems to be his trouble? I see, I see. Well, if you'll have a chair, the doctor will see you —" "Hello, Dr. Baldwin's Animal Hospital —"

In addition to everything else she'd learned, this summer, she'd learned to "meet the public," as the saying went. Secretly, she rather enjoyed the dulcet telephone voice she'd developed, and, to be honest, when it came to poise and charm in dealing with clients, she felt that they could not but be pleasantly impressed.

"Hello, Dr. Baldwin's Animal Hosp —" Her jaw dropped wide. The telephone froze in her fist.

Suddenly, in sheer reflex panic, the delightfully composed receptionist sprang from her chair. It was all she

156

could do to keep from clambering bodily onto the desk. For through the door and across the tiles came padding a tawny and quite terrifying beast. It had flat yellow eyes, a pure-white belly, and the tip of its heavy tail was black.

"I — I — I — there must be some mistake! I — I — I'm sorry, but this is a small animal h-h-hospital — " She dragged her fascinated eyes to the distinguished-looking, gray-haired man who was leading the creature on a leash. " Of course, if you want to get in touch with Dr. Baldwin," she tried to assure him in a polite squeak, " I — I'm sure she'll be glad to treat it — it — this — this — "

" Puma! "

" To treat your puma at your house. But, really, I do think the — the best thing for you to do would be to get in touch with Dr. Miller, the superintendent of the zoo."

" My dear young lady," the man informed her in ringing tones, "I am Dr. Miller! "

Chapter 15
_____

TRACEY HAD NEVER SEEN the office clear so fast. All the chairs, filled with people and pets a moment ago, were now as empty as if a tornado had swept through.

Shamefacedly she edged toward the door. " I — I'll call Dr. Baldwin," she gulped.

Jane Baldwin came out, wearing an amused and interested expression. "Well, Doctor, this is an honor." She stood a respectful distance from the beast. " And who might this be? "

" How are you, Jane? This is Evelyn, the puma I told you Mrs. Miller has been raising since infancy for me. Isn't she a beauty? "

"She certainly is a healthy specimen — I'll say that. What seems to be the trouble?"

"Oh, nothing with Evelyn! I brought her along so you could see her. But we've got a little problem out at the zoo. Jupiter, one of our lions, got his tail broken in a cage door. And Dr. Gerwin, our regular vet, is laid up with the flu. I wonder if you're too busy to take a run out and do the job for me."

"Well, frankly, these are my office hours."

"Oh, no hurry, no hurry! We can wait till you're through."

The doctor cast a glance around the now-deserted room. Winking at Tracey, she gave a little shrug. "The way things look around here, however, it wouldn't make much difference. Besides, I'm giving a party tonight for one of my girls — I'd just as soon leave early. O.K., wait'll I get my bag of tools."

Tracey hadn't moved. There was a queer prickling all over her skin, and her throat felt like cold, dry flannel. But she had an intense longing to stroke that sleek hide. How smooth it was, like a good heavy bolt of dust-colored satin! The throat and the inside of the legs as well as the belly, she saw now, were also snow white. The muscles rippled. A dim rumbling came from deep within it, but not ominously — more the contented throb of a cat's purring. Its whiskers were long and delicate, like pen strokes. It gave off a musty but rather tart, pleasant odor, and its eyes were cold yellow jewels set a little slantwise in the exquisitely sculptured face. It was fascinating; it was marvelous and rather awful to look at up so close.

"You like wild animals?" the famous zoo director asked.

"I — I've always thought so. I've never been this close to one before. Unless you'd count a baby ocelot we had

158

in here earlier this summer, and he, poor little guy, was almost too little and sick to count."

When Dr. Baldwin returned, her professional bag in hand, Whit was hard on her heels. Oddly enough, in view of his frank aversion to Butch, the look he gave the puma was one of joyous admiration. "I had to come see her, Sir. What's her name? Mind if I pet her?"

"Evelyn. No, go right ahead — she's very friendly."

Whit knelt and caressed the tawny flanks. His throat was working oddly, his face, as he rose, was alive with a single hope. And even before he voiced his request Tracey hoped with all her heart that Dr. Baldwin would grant it.

"Look, we're not too busy now — how about taking me along to help?"

The doctor, fishing car keys from her purse, regarded him an instant, then her eyes turned thoughtfully to Tracey. "Not this time, Whit — I'm sorry," she said decisively. "You're needed too much right here. But, Tracey, I'm taking you."

"Me?" Tracey gasped.

"Yes, if you'll hurry. Get out of that apron and grab your purse. I'll drop you off home when we're through. Whit, you take charge. Tell everybody we won't be back."

Tracey was too overcome to more than glance at her madly mixed emotions. Already stripping off the apron, she tore through back rooms and up the steel staircase. "I'm going to the zoo! she announced to Jake, Bert, and everybody else in her path. "Dr. Baldwin's going to let me help set a lion's tail!"

And this would give Diane just that much more chance to re-enslave Whit, if that's what she was really up to. And being Diane, she probably was — Tracey had sense enough to recognize that. And Whit would never forgive her for cutting him out like this. Because girls should never compete with men, or get ahead of them in any way, especially in their professions — not if you hoped to enslave one of them yourself. But it was all too hopeless anyway, because Whit would never, never, no matter what he said, get over Diane.

Yet all these very real concerns faded behind the reality of this glorious chance. She didn't know when she'd been so awed, excited, honored, or deliciously scared to death. As the doctor backed her handsome Cadillac expertly out of the exercise building, where she kept it, and Tracey climbed in beside her, her thoughts darted feverishly ahead.

Dr. Baldwin must be taking her along for assistance, surely, but — to just what — extent? Would she be expected to hold the — the lion's head, perhaps, during the anesthetic? climb with her employer right into the cage?

She'd have died rather than ask, however: if Dr. Baldwin suspected how madly her heart was pounding, she might turn back and take Whit instead. And to Tracey's own stubborn, rather impish surprise, she discovered that however she adored him, she wasn't ready to give up this chance.

The doctor herself seemed in high good humor as she drove through the park. "Good old Dr. Miller!" she laughed. "He would pick one of our busiest days to do me a favor like this."

"Do you a favor?" Tracey asked.

"That's the way I look at it. He knows it can get a little monotonous treating domestic animals, and how fond I am of those big cats."

"Aren't you scared?" Tracey dared to ask.

"Sure, a little. That caudal nerve that goes down any animal's tail is the most sensitive thing there is. That lion has probably licked his tail raw, and I doubt if he'll be

160

in an exactly benevolent mood." Tracey shuddered as the doctor went on. "Fear's a natural emotion, like pain, given us for our own protection. But when working with animals the thing is not to show it. You've got to demonstrate by your actions that you're the boss. Speak in a stern tone of voice, and make every move definite."

"I — I'll try to remember," Tracey said shakily. "My goodness, the zoo's lucky they have you to call on when their own vet is sick."

The woman at the wheel gave a dry, mischievous little laugh. "Oh, no, as I said before, Dr. Miller's doing me a favor. He has several competent aids out here who could do this job." She turned into the entrance marked Zo-LOGICAL PARK. "And I may as well warn you some of them will probably stand around and scoff."

"Scoff?" Tracey protested, aghast.

"Sure — make snide remarks. Because I'm a woman. And women, it is well-known, don't belong around the big stuff. That's one reason I chose you to accompany me instead of Whit. You're both interested in large animals, but Whit's been with me on jobs like this before. You haven't — you can use the experience."

She approached the hoofed-stock area, where some bison and mountain goats were grazing, drew up before a stone building near the prong-horned antelopes. "What's more to the point," said Dr. Baldwin, slamming the car door behind her, "you might as well get used to what we gals are up against."

Dr. Miller, who had disposed of Evelyn somewhere, was waiting inside. "Good, good! I see you didn't get tied up in too much traffic. Jupiter's right this way. Sorry this zoo doesn't have a proper hospital — that's where he should be. But the boys have put him in a squeeze cage to keep him from rooting around too much."

161

He led the way past other cages where "the boys," as he called the attendants, were busy with other animals. It was feeding time, and the place rang and echoed with a savage excitement. There was a tart, metallic, almost citric taste of excitement on the air. Dread and joy were shoving for space in Tracey's chest as they approached the massive beast, which lay sullen behind its confining bars. There was barely room for him to rise, but at the sight of them he got to his feet, the great leathery lips curled back, and a snarl that sounded like the ripping of an electric saw split the air.

"Hey, Jupiter! Hey there, boy! Take it easy. This is Dr. Baldwin, who's going to patch up that tail," Dr. Miller said in brusque tones.

He turned to her where she stood, small and trim in her tailored summer suit, calmly looking the situation over. Already a couple of young male uniformed attendants had dropped their activities and were sauntering up, trying to restrain expressions of skeptical amusement.

"This is Dr. Baldwin, boys. She's in charge, and I want you to give her all the assistance she needs."

"Oh, you bet! Yes, Sir," one of them grinned, exchanging glances with his friend, while Tracey seethed.

"Hello, fellows." Dr. Baldwin's voice was friendly as she occupied herself with opening her case. "If you'll just get me a table to work on. I think I'll give him a local," she told Dr. Miller.

"Want them to rope a paw?"

"No, thanks," she said crisply, and Tracey secretly cheered. Dr. Baldwin would show these detractors how little she needed them. "I'll give him a shot." She turned to inform Tracey, "That gluteus muscle isn't very big in a lion, but it's big enough."

The wheeled metal table came rumbling up, and she

prepared the shot. Jupiter, meanwhile, sensing pain, had opened his cavernous jaws and was roaring loud enough to be heard clear to the White House. The fact that he could not literally lunge his way through the confining bars did not minimize the general impression of heinous threat. Tracey clung desperately to the edge of the cold white metal table. Worst of all was the wickedly alert way the men were watching not only the capable small doctor but Tracey herself. I won't disgrace her! she vowed grimly, setting her teeth. I will act cool, calm, and collected if it kills me.

"My, my, aren't we noisy though?" Dr. Baldwin lifted her face to Jupiter to comment. "Well, I don't blame you — nobody likes a hypo." And weak though Tracey was, she could have applauded at the brisk, controlled way her idol strode to the cage.

Then an acutely embarrassing reality presented itself. For some reason, the squeeze cage was elevated several feet. The lion was a large one and the muscle the doctor wanted was not quite within her reach.

"I'm sorry." Dr. Baldwin turned, the trace of an embarrassed smile flicking her face. "I'm afraid you'll have to get me something to stand on."

At that the laughter that the men had been suppressing burst out. It mingled with the enraged bellowing of the beast. And though flustered, Dr. Baldwin joined in. "Here, how's this?" With a gesture of exaggerated gallantry, one of the men placed a box at her feet.

"That's fine." The doctor mounted, in one quick motion made the injection, sprang down. "No, no, don't take it away — that was just a tranquilizer. He'll be calmer in a few minutes; we'll anesthetize him then."

Within ten minutes Jupiter, king of the beasts, lay placid, a peace-loving lion whose poor, battered tail was being mended, and who couldn't care less. They had simply pulled it through the bars and laid it on the table. Tracey helped the doctor prepare the splint — a piece of plaster-of-Paris-impregnated gauze soaked in warm water. Expertly the doctor worked, shaping it around the injured member. Fascinated, Tracey stood at her shoulder, watching.

She was still very much aware of the men, who hung about, grinning, making cracks behind their hands, obviously hoping to goad this woman into a blunder. Obviously, they couldn't see, or didn't want to, the skill, the sureness, of those strong supple fingers. But even they could not deny the speed with which the whole operation was accomplished.

In a scant half hour Jupiter's tail was back in his cage with him and the table being trundled off. Dr. Baldwin seemed a trifle tired but triumphant. "Well! Now if he just doesn't chew the cast off — "

"Oh, he won't — we'll see to that," Dr. Miller told her. "Won't we, boys? Matter of fact," he informed Tracey, as their heels rang on the stone floor, walking back, "a lion will show very good sense about his tail. Jupiter'll probably worry that cast a little bit, but he'll know it's there for protection, and it'll make him careful not to lash that tail around or get it caught in another door."

They came out into the late-afternoon light, shook hands. Fathers in sports shirts and mothers in sunback dresses were leading or carrying children toward their cars. The smell of hot dogs and peanuts mingled with the rank smell of animals and trampled grass. Tracey felt tired too now — after all, it had been an emotionally exhausting day — but stimulated, keyed to some keen and volatile new pitch.

"Thank you, Dr. Miller," she tried to express it. "I

164

mean — it's meant a lot to me to meet you and get to see some of the zoo work backstage like this."

"Oh, don't thank me," he chuckled, "Thank your boss. She's the expert. Have her bring you around again sometime. For that matter, come around yourself any time you want to learn something."

"I will, believe me," Tracey said. "'I'll take you up on that.'"

"Now where?" The doctor merged with the flow of cars across the Calvert Street Bridge. "Shall I drop you off at your aunt's?"

"If it's not out of your way. You've probably got a lot of things to do for the party tonight."

"Oh, not too much. I'm going to keep it simple. By the way, what did you get Diane?"

"Diane!" Tracey jerked upright, clapping a hand to her open mouth. "Oh, good heavens! I forgot I'm the committee to pick out her present. I was going to shop right after work. If we come to a luggage store that's still open, you'd better let me off."

"Luggage? That's a good idea. And luggage might be a good idea for Whit too."

"Whit?" Tracey gasped. She felt suddenly faint. She felt far worse than when she had stood beside the lion's cage. "Why Whit?"

"He's going to be leaving us shortly too. He didn't want me to say anything until it was settled. But he's finally been reconciled with his mother."

"His mother?" Tracey's voice sounded feeble; she hoped the doctor didn't notice anything. "Oh, I'm so glad. It — it should make a big difference in him."

"Yes. Yes, I think it's an awfully good thing. For one thing, she has money, and she's going to send him back to vet school where he belongs."

"Where?" Tracey asked, and her anxiety was plain. For one ghastly instant she was convinced the doctor would say Iowa State, with Diane.

"Ontario. It's the oldest veterinary college on the North American Continent. I'm convinced it's the best place for him. I've been pulling all kinds of strings to get him in."

"That's — wonderful," Tracey said thinly. "I'm — awfully glad for him!"

Blindly she got out when the doctor pulled up before a leather goods store in Georgetown whose lights were still on. Numbly she forced herself to pick out a small smartly fitted train case for Diane.

Chapter 16

SHE HAD TO TELL DUD — she couldn't help it. In spite of the party, in spite even of this devastating news about Whit, she couldn't resist phoning him.

Sandwich in one hand, party shoes in the other, she paused on the stairway landing to dial. "Listen, I can't talk but a minute, but guess what happened to me this afternoon?" Before he could answer she went on: "I went to the zoo with Dr. Baldwin and Dr. Miller himself, no less, and helped set a lion's tail!"

There was an instant of appreciative silence. Then an even more appreciative whistle. "No kiddin', Trace? Yow-e-e-e-e!"

"Well, actually, I didn't help much, but I was there — that's the main thing. And Dr. Miller invited me back."

"Hey, now look! That's great, y'know it? Boy! Do I envy you!"

"Listen, what're you doing tonight?" she asked, on impulse. Dr. Baldwin had suggested she invite Dudley if she wanted to. She hadn't. Not before. She'd been too preoccupied with her campaign to get somewhere with Whit. But suddenly she was drawn to Dud, won by his endearing and spontaneous reaction to her news. And, to look at it in a practical light, whose shoulder could she cry on after Whit went away? For that matter, she thought grimly, it wouldn't hurt to have a male beside her tonight, even a plain guy like Dudley.

Because, looking back on the day, she wanted to kick herself for the way she'd lost perspective on Diane. How could Tracey have been such a stupe as to misread her motives even for a minute? When Diane acted that way around a man she had but one aim in mind — to bag him. What she intended to do with him, especially since they both were leaving and she was supposed to be serious about Jeff, was anybody's guess. But then girls as beautiful as Diane didn't have to have reasons. Anyway, having neatly scooped Whit back into her net, Diane would probably have them both flapping at her side tonight.

Dud, however, demurred when Tracey told him about the party. "Aaaah, you'd better not bother with me. You'd better keep it to people who work down there."

"Dud, please," she urged, suddenly convinced that she couldn't survive the affair without him. "I realize it's awfully late to be asking, but I — need you."

"Well, since you put it like that," he said, and to her dismay she detected a certain reluctance. "What'll I wear?"

"That's a good question." She hadn't thought much about this phase of it herself. "Nothing too dress-uppy. How about that tweed sports jacket I always liked you in?"

"I didn't know you ever liked me in anything."

"Oh, don't be difficult!" she scolded. It was annoying to have good old Dud, who'd always been so dependable, start adding to her troubles tonight. "You know — it's kind of tannish brown and with little coppery dots in it that match the coppery dots in your eyes."

"Dots news to me," he cracked disgustingly, though she laughed in spite of herself. "I mean dot you ever noticed the color of my eyes. O.K., now I'll tell you what to wear — your Swiss cheese."

"My what?"

"That yellow dress with the holes in it. Eyelets, I guess you call 'em."

"Oh, but that's too fancy."

"It's the best-looking thing I ever saw you in. I mean, you're the best-looking thing I ever saw in it. And remember how you told me this guy Whit never got to see you in anything but an apron covered with dog hairs? Well, here's your chance to look really doggy for him."

Tracey was taken aback. She jerked the phone from her ear and stood ruminating a second. Dud was smart. Too smart sometimes. So he was not forgetting the fact that she was still smoldering with unrequited love for Whit! But did he have to dump new fuel on the fire and fan it so baldly as all that? It made her feel like a fool and a bit of a louse besides.

"Who cares?" she demanded, and the incredible fact of it stabbed her with new impact. "He's — leaving town himself next week."

"Then all the more reason," Dud argued. "But if you don't want to wear it for him, Trace, wear it for me," he asked simply. "Please."

She was trapped. There was no getting out of it. Dud could be stubborn on occasion. And it seemed absolutely vital to her now that she have him for moral support. Also, she sensed that this meant a lot to him. It would be too brutal to hurt his feelings. Heaven knows, she'd hurt him enough already in ways she didn't mean to.

Oh, how did she manage to back herself into corners like this?

She ran on upstairs and yanked the dress out of the closet. Holding it up against her, she studied it in the mirror. It was really an awfully good dress, bought on sale at Jelleff's. And she'd grown since she'd worn it last spring: it was now just about right for an informal length. Except for the full skirt and the truly exquisite material, it wasn't too fancy — she guessed.

Still, showering and trying to do something about her hair, she was doubtful. When her hair was wet and could be slicked behind her ears, it really looked terrific and sophisticated in a way that was oddly right with the dress. But the minute it started to dry it shot up in all directions, and it dried fast. In sheer desperation, Tracey caught up a pair of fingernail scissors and was about to whack off more when her mother came to the rescue with a brush and a can of spray.

By some magic, her mother got it subdued into a respectable fringe bob and browbeat her into wearing the black velvet headband. " It makes me look so demure! " Tracey protested, glowering.

" It's a demure kind of dress," her mother said. " Really, Tracey, Dudley's right — you look marvelous in it."

Ha! Tracey thought. Nobody could possibly look marvelous in the same room with Diane. But still Dud might be right: if this dress did anything for her, she owed it to herself to give all interested parties a chance to see her in it. And that included not only Whit but Jeff Carter.

The nearer they drew to the handsome apartment hotel where Dr. Baldwin lived, however, the more her courage

169

waned; the more she yearned for a safe, comfortable cotton. It would be simply too disastrous if that's what Diane and Dr. Baldwin were wearing. Oh, why hadn't she pocketed her pride and called up Diane to find out?

"Some swell dump, huh?" Dudley admired as they walked across the big softly lighted chrome-and-marble lobby, their feet sinking into the deep wine carpeting. He rang for the elevator. "This is the kind of spread you'll be having when you're rich and famous from setting lions' tails."

Tracey laughed to conceal her mounting nervousness. She'd always dreaded parties. And the nearer she got to this one, the more she wished she'd worked up a good old-fashioned headache and stayed safely home reading a good book on hoof-and-mouth disease or something. Now that the hour was approaching she didn't see how she could stand it, seeing Diane with both Whit and Jeff signed, sealed, and delivered into her keeping before she left. And to make it all the more unbearable, Tracey would probably be the only person all dressed up. If she were, she'd never speak to Dudley Wallace again!

They padded down the hushed corridor. Dud lifted the tiny knocker. The door opened, and Tracey was so relieved she almost hugged her boss. For Dr. Baldwin stood there looking absolutely stunning in a low-cut, wheat-colored raw silk. And behind her were a couple of other girls, who had once worked for the hospital, both in party dresses. While Mrs. Phillips, who was presiding over the punch bowl, was a froth of pink chiffon.

Diane alone, standing deep in conversation beside the pleated, floor-length draperies with Jeff, wore a simple white-linen sun back. "You're no friend," she chided, holding out a hand. "Why didn't somebody warn me this was going to be white tie and tails?"

170

"We felt this was an occasion, we — wanted to do you the honor," Tracey consoled her, feeling the slight advantage of being accidentally right for once. Not that it mattered. Diane would still have been the most ravishing girl in the room if she'd worn blue jeans. "After all, you don't need glad rags to make you gorgeous. Give the rest of us a chance."

"You're too sweet." Diane emitted her mocking little trill of a laugh. But she gave Tracey a look of surprised and honest appraisal. "While we're dishing it out, though, you're terrific in that dress." With the bland, twinkling, proprietary air of a girl so assured she can afford to be generous, she turned to Jeff. "Isn't she, darling?"

"I'll say! Hi, Tracey! I've been trying to get in the good word myself. Watch out — some guy'll be after you, but fast."

"Some guy?" Dudley sauntered up. "Watch your language! That's me, pal. I already am." The two boys shook hands. "But she sure gave me a hard time getting her to wear it."

"That's nothing to the hard time he gave me getting him to come," Tracey retorted.

"Well, Dudley, hello! Let's not argue about it — let's just be thankful you succeeded!" Diane was regarding Dudley with such a sudden, shining look of sweet intrigue that Tracey was brought up short.

Diane, she realized, startled, saw something in Dudley she'd missed. Hey, now! she thought, protesting. And, blinking, she drew back to take a better look at him herself. He'd certainly filled out this summer: that gangling, kid-scientist look had somehow gotten lost in the neck and shoulders of a young man. And he'd acquired a most becoming tan. That job trimming trees he'd had, maybe that had done it — all that climbing up in the sun. What-

171

ever it was, Diane was finding no objection to it at all! And though Tracey was belatedly proud and infinitely grateful, she was also a trifle irked and on guard. After all, Diane had already pretty well cleaned her out of men. And even if she didn't want Dud herself, he was not going to be one more conquest for Diana to scoop up, yes, and possibly hurt even in the scant time she had left.

Feeling rather agreeably like a dog in a manger, Tracey took his arm. "Let's go get some punch."

"Lunch, punch, crunch — that's all this dame thinks of," Dud rudely said. "Say, you coming back to Washington to work next summer, Diane?"

"Who knows?" She shrugged. Her eyes lingered with an appealing plaintiveness first on him, then on Jeff. "Life's so unpredictable for a girl, especially when she's unpredictable herself. Also, it's no fair!" she protested. "Every time I get my mind made up, somebody tries to change it."

Jeff gave a love-troubled smile. His arm encircled her tiny waist. He flashed a rather comradely look of entreaty to Tracey and shook his head. "And just when I think I've got it changed for keeps, she turns around and changes it back again."

"Well, good," Tracey said bluntly, avoiding his eyes. "Diane's got to finish vet school — she's just got to. People shouldn't go around trying to get her to do anything else. Say," she asked tactlessly, to change the subject, "where's Whit?"

Instantly she regretted it. For instantly, like something tangible, she could feel the tension that came over everyone, especially Diane.

"Yes, where is he? It's getting late. What time is it?" Diane consulted her watch. "Why, it's nearly ten o'clock. If he blackballs my party, if he doesn't show up to tell me good-by, I — I'll never speak to him again! "

"Oh, he'll surely be here." Tracey could scarcely keep the sudden anxiety out of her own voice. He had to come. She couldn't endure it if he didn't. Even the pain of seeing them together would not be as bad as not seeing him at all. "Why, my goodness, he wouldn't dream of missing it."

As, of course, he wouldn't, she knew with a dumb pang. However much it would hurt him to have to join people in telling Diane good-by, he'd come because he couldn't help it any more than he could help loving her. But whatever his reasons for coming, he must, must come, or the whole evening would be ruined!

"But, then, even if he doesn't show up, I'll understand," Diane amended her own threat with a soft, secretive little air. "He's under some pressures. He's — well, making plans of his own, which I'm not at liberty to reveal."

"Why all the mystery?" Tracey asked, annoyed. "Dr. Baldwin told me herself he's going to Ontario, the vet school, to finish his own training. I mean — certainly she wouldn't have told me if it were any deep, dark secret."

Diane's brows shot up: she looked vexed and taken aback. "Well, yes, but that's only part of it. He's confided a lot of things to me that definitely aren't common knowledge." She glanced at her wrist again and then restlessly about the room. "Oh, well, who cares? Jeff, let's sample the punch."

"Now you can have yours, baby." Dud grinned amiably at Tracey, and they followed the other couple across the sculptured white carpeting.

It was strange seeing Dr. Baldwin in this unaccustomed setting. Tracey had no idea she had such excellent taste. Oyster-white walls set off the striking modern oil paintings. A huge walk-in window overlooking the park dis-

173

played her collection of rare Lutz glass. Most of the furniture was in shades of lemon or rich brown, accented with touches of brilliant cerise. Flowers were everywhere, and whole walls given over to books. It was indeed an opulent and lovely place.

Even stranger was seeing the hospital staff in civilized coats and ties instead of the usual spattered aprons, and meeting their husbands and wives. But strangest of all to notice how the other girls present were watching Dud. This was definitely going to take some getting used to, Tracey thought, amazed.

The door kept opening and more people arriving. Dr. Baldwin had invited former employees and their families who had known Diane. The tempo of the greetings, the well wishes, and the reminiscences increased. And again and again you heard the surprised question, "Where's Whit?" And Diane's reply was a bit defensive too: " Oh, he'll be here. He'd better be! Of course, he's awfully busy. He's leaving too, did you know? Going to Canada to finish off his veterinary training. Isn't that marvelous? "

And there was a faint note of triumph in her voice, or so it seemed to Tracey, shifting from foot to foot in her seldom-worn high heels and watching Dud being just too, too amusing for those stupid girls, even as she also watched the door. Oh, Whit! Where are you? Is it really this bad for you, that you can't take it — coming to tell Diane good-bye with the rest of us?

And Diane, angry though she pretended to be with him, would know it. And whatever disappointment she felt, for Diane was disappointed — it communicated itself to Tracey like some wretched secret bond — Diane would be appeased by the smug, unshatterable knowledge: he was hers. No matter how she treated him or how far away he

174

too went, he would always belong to her. And yet it was fortunate at that, that he would also be safely far away from a silly girl like Tracey Temple, who might be tempted to try to comfort him in his loss.

Dr. Baldwin, looking flushed and pleased, yet rather concerned, made her way to Tracey. "I'm afraid something's happened to Whit. I think maybe we'd better go ahead with the gift, don't you?"

"Yes, if you think so. It's getting late."

Tracey followed the doctor into the bedroom where the package was hidden, but protested firmly when Dr. Baldwin asked her to make the presentation speech. "After all, everybody else has known her longer than I have." So they got Bert, who hammered on the grand piano for attention and was ineloquent but very funny, telling jokes not only on Diane but on all of them.

"Oh, what a beauty!" Diane cried, joyfully tearing aside the wrappings. She lifted the lovely case for all to see. "I'll have to say you shouldn't have done it, but I'm certainly glad you did. In fact, I feel like curling up in a corner and having a good cry!" She caught her breath then, and her eyes actually filled.

Following them, Tracey felt her own heart leap. For Whit had slipped in. In all the attention that had been focused on Diane, no one had noticed. Anyway, there he was, leaning against the wall, arms folded, his stern chin jutted, but a look of almost wicked buoyancy on his handsome face.

"Whit!" Clinging to Jeff with one hand, the case with the other, Diane scurried toward him. "Look, just look! Isn't it gorgeous?"

Grinning boldly at Jeff, Whit stroked his jaw. "Gorgeous is not exactly the adjective I'd pick."

"You nut! I don't mean him — I mean this! You couldn't have given me anything nicer or that I need more. Thank you so much."

"Hey, now, not so fast! Don't thank me! "

"Well, but of course — I mean — you had a part in it."

"Don't be too sure. I haven't paid my two bucks yet." Still wearing that sardonic but oddly chipper grin, Whit had roused. He turned away, began shaking hands with other people. And it was strange, it was just too — impossible, yet Tracey had the distinct impression that all this was different from the bitter way he had sometimes taunted Diane. The times when he was really suffering over her. But it was too sudden. She didn't dare trust her own judgment. Maybe she was imagining it because this was the way she wanted it to be.

"Well, he finally showed up," Dud remarked beside her. There was something rather resigned and cryptic in his voice. "Now I guess your evening's a success."

"Oh, Dud, don't be like that! " she snapped. She hadn't thought he suspected. "You seem to have been enjoying yourself."

"Sure, why not? In fact, if you'll excuse me, I think I'll go amuse myself some more by passing the nuts."

"Dud, wait! " Absurdly, she felt weak. She wanted him beside her when Whit spotted her — which he had. He was making his way to her, a puzzled quirk to his thick brows.

"Pardon me, but haven't we met someplace before? "

"Whit! " She stood stupidly shaking. "Where've you been? I — we've been so afraid you wouldn't come."

He was circling slowly around her, the old, wry, derisive look on his face. Yet something new had been added — this exciting air of buoyancy and freedom that you could feel emanating from him like a force.

176

"The face is familiar, but the figure — Oh, yeah, I know!" He snapped his fingers. "It must've been there all the time. Under a flea-bitten apron. The hair, though, I don't understand. It's tame as a kitten: it's actually lying down!"

She swallowed; her throat hurt. "Stop making fun of me, Whit," she begged.

"Making fun?" He halted abruptly. "I'm only trying to tell you in my own inimitable way that you look like two million dollars. Or maybe it's because I feel like a couple of million myself."

"Look! You paid me a compliment and you're stuck with it," she warned. "Not that I'm not glad that you feel so good. I must say, though, I'm flabbergasted! I mean —" She gestured toward the group that included Jeff and Diane. "Well, it's the last thing I expected."

"Oh, that!" He laughed curtly and ran a hand through his curly hair. It had been newly cut, she noticed. Everything about him seemed somehow sharpened, trimmed, revitalized. "Frankly, I almost forgot to come. Y'see, I've already been spending the evening with one beautiful woman."

"Your mother? You mean she's here?" Tracey exclaimed.

"She was. I just put her on the plane."

"Oh. So that's what Diane meant."

"Diane? What does she know about it? I didn't even know Mother was coming myself until after work."

Diane was descending upon them then, laughing and little and lovely, but her eyes had a determined glow. "My goodness, can't I turn my back without being talked about? Whit, let's find a cozy corner — you and I have a few loose ends to sew up."

"Loose ends?" Whit was gripping Tracey's shoulder.

177

She felt a slight but definite shudder go through him. "Listen, baby, all loose ends in my life have been whacked off tonight, but good."

"But, Whit — " Diane bit her firm little flower of a lip. Her eyes, still radiant, narrowed slightly, went flat. "You will be at the plane to see me off in the morning? "

"Honey, in the morning tell the pilot to dip over my diggings, where I'll be deep in the sack. I leave all the final fond farewells to Jeff."

"I assure you he'll be happy to hear that! " Diane said tightly. Head high, she left. In a few minutes, however, she came whisking back. Tracey marveled at the serenity of her even now — the bland, sparkling, absolute confidence — reminding him: "You know where I'll be. You have my address. And I'll have yours before long. Goodby, Whit. Jeff and I are leaving now."

Whit's fingers gripped Tracey's arm so much tighter she winced. "So are we," he muttered. "Let's get out of here. I'll flag a cab."

"I'm sorry, Whit — " Oh, if she'd only known! "I came with Dud."

"Dud? Oh, yeah, the white-rat lad. Well, tell him it's an emergency. Tell him you had to go back to the zoo — that lion had a relapse. Tell him anything. He won't mind."

"Oh, but he will! That's the trouble — he's got feelings too, like me. And I can't bear to hurt them. Besides, he — he's not just a white-rat lad! "

"Florence, Florence, don't tell me you're falling for the guy! "

"No, but it's not fair of you to be so condescending."

"O.K., O.K., tell you what I'm gonna do — " He signaled to Dudley, who came up agreeably, munching peanuts. "Hi, Dud! Would you be a good Joe and let me ride home with you and Trace? To her place, I mean."

Dudley didn't hesitate. "Why, sure." A faint grin touched his mouth as he read Tracey's nakedly anxious face. His own eyes were without reproach. "Any old time you're ready to go."

The two boys visited amiably all the way. And when they drew up under the archaic porte-cochere, Dud simply leaned over and opened the door. "If you don't mind, I think I'll shove off. I've got a big day tomorrow amputating limbs from willow oaks."

They stood watching his taillights vanish swiftly down the drive. Then Whit and Tracey turned to each other.

"You don't have to go right in, do you?"

Tracey shook her head. It was late. If her mother had heard the car, she would also be listening for her footsteps, and wonder. But she must have this time, this small miraculous gift of time, alone with Whit tonight if it meant her very life.

Wordlessly, she went to the wrought-iron patio gate and lifted the latch.

Chapter 17

THE MOSSY STONES were damp and a trifle slippery underfoot. There was a smell of mint and leaf mold and the bittersweet odor of geraniums in their ornate stone pots. A round, late minx of a moon had come rolling up over the cemetery slopes, penciling everything clearly — benches, and a dribbling fountain, and the sundial — in fluorescent strokes of silver. Its light poured down through the tall maple trees, reprinting all in a heady contrast of trembling light and inky shadow.

179

They sat down on a weathered stone seat, the ends of which were the shape of prancing griffins. Gargoyles grinned at them from the walls, and icons, half choked in ivy, stood, mysterious, in their niches.

Whit whistled softly. " You've been holding out on me. I had no idea your relatives were so rich! "

" Rich and crazy," she told him, trying to keep her teeth from chattering. "It's my great-aunt. We're just the poor relations, and I'm sort of house doctor to the cats."

As if to confirm her statement, one of them appeared, specterlike, along the ledge, howled plaintively, and flowed on into the moonlight. The yellow eyes of two others gleamed and vanished.

" Speaking of cats, I could have killed you for beating me out on that trip to the zoo."

" I know you could."

" But I'm also glad you got the chance."

" I — I guess I sort of know that too."

" I hope you do," he said sternly. " Lousy as I've been to you, Tracey, I don't want to go away without making sure you understand one thing: I believe in your future as a vet. Nothing will make me any happier than knowing you make good."

Nothing! Nothing more than that? But she must settle for what was in his heart to give. For Whit it was a good deal, at that.

" You haven't been lousy to me, Whit — you've been grand."

" I've been not only lousy: I've been lousy-lousy, and you know it. Hey, you're cold! Put your hand in my pocket; better yet, put my coat on." Over her protests he stripped it off, and she sat hugging it to her, sniffing its smell of smooth satin lining and linen. She sat huddled into it as in an embrace.

180

"About my mother and why I missed the party. She called last week to say she'd send me back to school if I still wanted to go. To tell the truth, Tracey, I was upset. I wasn't sure that I wanted to take her money, or even if I wanted to go back! We talk big sometimes, but come right down to it I have a good berth here with Doc. I guess I've even enjoyed feeling sorry for myself as the thwarted young genius playing second fiddle to a woman! Anyway, it took some stiff talking on Dr. Baldwin's part to make me see the light."

"I wish you'd told me, Whit."

"I didn't tell anybody — I was too ashamed."

"Not even Diane?"

"Are you kidding? She's the last person to whom I'd admit a thing like that."

"I suppose." Because he was still so desperately in love with her, Tracey was reasoning. Because he'd have too much pride: he'd want his beloved to see in him only the best.

"She'd never have understood. I think maybe you would have — or do, Tracey. Young as you are you've got a lot of understanding."

"I'm not so young," she flashed. "Anyway, people say I'm old for my age."

"You're very, very young and very sweet. And you've got years of college ahead of you, years of work and studying and falling in and out of love with boys."

"I don't fall out so easy, Whit."

He gave a short little laugh and sprang up. Hands in his pockets, he stood, one foot planted on the bench, his mocking face challenging the moon.

"You'd better learn, kid," he warned her. "You'd better learn fast. It's no good loving too hard. There's too much misery in it — don't I know that? Well, I'm free of it at

181

last. Y'know, that's one thing my mother did for me to-night. It's a bigger present than the check she wrote." He lowered his gaze, nodding as if in wondering agreement with himself. " She doesn't know it but she did that for me too: she brought about my release."

" I don't get it."

" Well, she's my mother, see? and I love her. She's beautiful and spoiled, but I love her, which makes me miserable. But I can't help it: it — it's a kind of biological law. But there's no law that says I've got to go out and ask for more misery by being in love with somebody else beautiful and spoiled. My mother — boy! Am I glad she came and that I found out how much I really love her, after all! Because, I know it sounds crazy, but it's the very best possible cure for ever loving another beautiful girl! "

" But not for — love. Not for just plain loving, Whit! "

He lifted her chin. " Who said anything about wanting a cure for that? "

The stars paused in their courses, the moon smiled urgently; they could hear a bus whooshing by at the foot of the hill, and the cicadas like little ghosts rattling chains in the trees. Please! — Tracey was pleading in a soft and terrible ecstasy deep in her soul. Oh, kiss me, please!

The moment lasted forever. And ended. Whit pulled her resolutely to her feet. " You'd better go in."

Whit didn't want a party. In fact, he had such a fit when somebody suggested it that they thought he was going to fling off his apron and stalk off then and there. But he was very sweet about the huge three-layer cake Mrs. Phillips brought in on his last day. And, though he didn't say much, obviously delighted with the book they had all chipped in to buy him.

" The *Infectious Diseases of Domestic Animals*. Just

what I wanted," he laughed. "No kidding. I'll study it on the train."

On the train! So soon now, so soon! His big sturdy bags were already packed and standing in the corner; the cab was on its way. And he'd given them all fair warning not to try to see him off. "I want to remember you just as you are," he claimed, and everybody laughed, because they all looked like the witches in *Macbeth* — it had been one of those hectic days.

The outer door opened. "Anybody here order a taxi?"

"Guilty," said Whit, beginning to shake hands. "Be with you in a minute."

Tracey suddenly couldn't bear it. To tell him good-by, just like that, in front of everybody. No, no, better not to say good-by to him at all! Blindly she grabbed up a stack of paper plates and plunged off through the swinging door. She pitched them out and ran, for comfort, to stand beside Cookie and the puppies' cage. She was crying, she couldn't help it, when she heard his heels come pounding after her.

"Hey, you! Cut that out."

"I'm sorry, Whit." She lowered her head, pressing her fingers tightly to her trembling mouth, fighting for control.

"Tracey," he said on impulse, whipping her about, "grab a lipstick, wash your face. We're getting out of here."

"Oh, Whit — Whit? You really want me?"

"Sure, why not? And while we're at it, we might's well take the family."

He had the puppy leashed and in his arms when Tracey came clacking back downstairs.

"Better tell the driver to hurry," Dr. Baldwin advised them. "You haven't too much time."

183

"Oh, we've got lots of time, haven't we, Tracey?"
Whit's eyes were flashing. She had never seen him so
charged with energy, so gay. He wrung the doctor's hand
a final time, and together they dashed out the door.

In the taxi he sat back playing with the puppy all the
way. "Now you be a good dog, hear?" he lectured. "Mind
your mamma and don't go running away." His eyes met
Tracey's forlorn ones. "She's a great little old mamma, our
Florence. The best little old dog taker-carer-of in the
world. Even if she hasn't gotten around to giving you a
name."

"Oh, I've named him all right," Tracey told him quietly.

"But you're not telling?"

She nodded. "You're not the only one can keep a secret
about a name."

He gazed at her long and tenderly. "Don't tell me you
named this mutt for me!"

"I love him," Tracey whispered. "I'll never forget that
he is — my family. And that I wouldn't have him except
for you."

"And I'll never forget you, Tracey. We'll write, we'll
keep in touch." Very gravely, then, he kissed her; leaning
over the squirming puppy to find her lips, he kissed her,
lightly, over and over, and his eyes had never been more
gentle or more sweet.

The cab stopped. They didn't stir for an instant. Not
until the driver announced loudly, "Union Station." And
climbing out to get the luggage, he slammed the door.

"Well" — Whit broke the spell — "We made it!" He
gave her back the puppy while he paid the driver, summoned a redcap. Hand in hand they hastened into the big
vaulted waiting room. Tracey held the dog desperately
close while Whit stood in line buying his ticket, comforted
by its wiggling warmth, by the hot, scratchy lick of the

tiny red tongue against her face. He understood already: he was kissing her too!

The big station clock said five minutes of the hour when Whit came rushing back; the announcer was already calling his train. Arms linked, they went onto the vast, echoing outer platform, hunting the proper gate. And they saw it, and it was open, and people were already crowding through.

"Well, Trace —" He halted, turned to her, the old sardonic grin on his mouth, but his gaze clear and grave. "Take care of yourself, study hard, work hard, and you'll have everything you've ever dreamed of someday. Your degree, your profession, your own practice, your ranch — everything. Nothing's impossible once you get off the dime, stop knocking yourself out over the wrong things. The things that were never really meant for you."

"But if nothing's impossible, Whit, then you can have everything! Everything!" she insisted fiercely. "And if you want something so much, doesn't that prove it's right for you?"

"No, honey. We can want the wrong things harder sometimes than the right ones. So much they foul us up, make us lose sight of our direction, lose the way."

The trainman was looking at them. "You going on the New York train, buddy? Better make it snappy, kiss her fast."

"Well, then — I guess I'd better." Whit lifted her chin. "Good-by, Tracey. Good-by, you wonderful kid." It was a strong kiss this time, firm and lasting. She would never forget it to her dying day. "Take care of our family."

He was running now. Through the gates, along the platform. She dashed blindly after him a little way. Then paused, with the screech of wheels in her ears, and it was like the pained outcry of her own spirit. He was climbing

185

up the moving steps now, disappearing.

But her eyes looked hungrily up and up, and she ran along beside the cars, and, oh, there he was, crowding along the aisle, and crouching, looking out as if for one last glimpse of her. And, pressing his hand to his mouth, he signaled a final caress. And that too she would file away with her treasures of this summer, to be lived over and over again in the coming days.

Dazedly, hugging the puppy, she turned back through the gates. She was crying, but she was happier than she had ever remembered being. Filled with a kind of glowing peace.

It was somehow no surprise to find Dudley wandering around the waiting room, alert for her. "I stopped by the hospital, and they told me you were here. I figured you might want a ride home. Hey, so this is the new dog? Mighty handsome little fellow. What breed?"

"A mutt. A — nobody. But I'll never have another dog I'll love like this."

"I know you won't," Dud said wisely. "And I don't blame you in the least."